Beyond the Code of Conduct

by

K.M. Daughters

Beyond the Code of Conduct

Cover Art by *Kim Mendoza*

The Wild Rose Press
PO Box 708
Adams Basin, NY 14410-0706
Visit us at www.thewildrosepress.com

Publishing History
First Crimson Rose Edition, 2009
Print ISBN: 1-60154-544-4

Published in the United States of America

"You want hot? I'll give you hot." In one swift motion she picked up a mug off the table and whipped it towards him, a perfect strike.

Lucky for him he still held his jacket in his hand. He swept it up like a toreador in front of his face. The coat took the brunt of the hit, but hot liquid splattered on his hands.

"Ouch. Damn. Stop it." He dropped the wet coat on the floor. His hands burned and he wiped them on his thighs to stop the heat. It had the opposite effect on his arousal.

Her eyes whipped around, apparently searching for something else to throw at him and tugged at the pillow on the back of the sofa. When it didn't give, she hopped up on the seat cushion and yanked at it harder. *If she realized how seductive she looked, she'd stop doing that.* A glimpse of lace panties made him groan.

"Honey, add a sorority sister and a little water on the front of your T-shirt and you have everyman's wet dream. You're killing me here."

The fury mounted on her face and he laughed.

She stepped down from the couch and stormed off to the kitchen.

"I'm sorry. I'm not laughing at you." No response from the kitchen.

Gathering together the launched items, he stacked the books and magazines on the coffee table and tucked her shoes beneath. He kicked off his shoes and placed them in a neat pair next to hers before settling on the couch.

It's fun to goad her. "While you're in there could you grab me a beer?"

Realizing a little too late why she had marched to the kitchen, a plate swished past inches from his ear and crashed against the bookcase.

Dedication

For My Nick and My Tom

ACKNOWLEDGMENT

How do we thank our talented editor, Joelle Walker,
without her editing our thank you? No red pen
allowed here, Joelle. Our deepest gratitude
to the gifted Joelle Walker for her insights,
her spot-on suggestions
and her unerring use of red-ink slashing.
You give us so much more than a better book.

Prologue

Johnny's deafening shriek ricocheted off of the trailer's tin walls and recoiled inside her head. She cringed.

"Shut him up, Becky." His growl was thick with menace that usually preceded a beating.

She flinched. "I'm trying, Daddy."

"I had a hard day," he said. "Last thing I need is that brat keeping me awake."

Daddy rolled over on the sofa bed, his back to her.

She held her wiggling, red-faced son close to her chest to muffle his annoying wails, but the heat from her body only brought louder squawks.

"That's it." The box springs creaked as he got up and swayed toward her. "I warned you over and over. No more, Becky. He goes."

He yanked the suddenly quiet baby out of her arms and lumbered toward the door of the trailer.

She sprang from the chair and followed. "Please Daddy! No!" she begged, trailing behind him.

Becky clawed at her father's undershirt-clad back as he carried the now screaming baby outside. "Where are you taking him?"

"Somewhere else." He shoved her away from the

cab of his dented brown truck, strapped the seatbelt around the flailing baby, and drove away.

Hysterically crying, Becky ran after the truck. Tears mixed with dust blinded her and she collapsed in the road.

The next morning her baby was still gone. The next afternoon she was gone.

It took her a few years but then daddy was gone, too.

Chapter 1

Bobbie Leighton huddled, miserable, in the compact rental car. The defroster and heater fan blasted tepid air in her face but did nothing to penetrate the biting cold. Her windows fogged more each time she exhaled a vaporous breath in the frigid cabin. Rubbing wet circles of condensation from the glass with her gloves, she watched for the arrival of the hearse-led procession at the cemetery.

The assignment that began with attendance at Jimmy Sullivan's funeral was logical, considering her history with the Sullivan family. None the less, she had begged the Special Agent in Charge to send someone else or, if for no other reason but to save the airfare, have a Special Agent in Chicago question the family.

Her boss was unyielding; the assignment was hers.

She wondered what kind of reception was in store for her, especially from Joe Sullivan. She chewed at the corner of her lip, fearing it would be as frosty as her windshield.

She shivered not only because of the lack of heat, but the chilling implications of Jimmy's death. He had been murdered, and if her agency's Intel was right, it might have had something to do with his connection with Bradley Sterling. The Sullivans wouldn't want her to prove that theory.

The memory of the woeful resonance of the bagpipes reverberating in the great cathedral at the funeral Mass was haunting. Mourners, most of them Chicago PD, had filled hundreds of rows of pews. Yet, only the hearse and two stretch limos glided past her parked car on the skinny road like huge ships sailing through a narrow strait.

The limos parked on the rise ahead of her and emptied with sounds like gunshots cracking the sub-zero air as doors were shoved closed. Six men, surely John Sullivan, his sons and son-in-law, stood in ready formation at the rear of the hearse prepared to carry Jimmy's casket to the gravesite. The three Sullivan women, arms linked, walked toward the grave, marked by a mound of frozen clods of grassy soil mixed with snow.

The pallbearers carried Jimmy toward his final rest, dark silhouettes against the pure white landscape and crystalline blue sky.

Bobbie turned off the engine and left the car. Feeling conspicuous as her boots crunched ice, she was careful not to tramp too heavily on the snow-crusted graves beneath her feet. She neared the group as the men eased the casket onto the interment scaffold. Heads snapped up and all eyes focused on Bobbie, the interloper at a private family funeral.

Jean Sullivan's eyes bored into her until she nodded in recognition and bowed her head again. Standing at Danny's right side, Molly's face bloomed with a smile and she stretched out her arm to encourage Bobbie to flank her in its welcoming circle. Bobbie fell in line.

"In the name of the Father and of the Son and of the Holy Spirit...."

The priest's intonations and sporadic nose sniffs,

the only sounds in their small, sorrowful world.

Pressed against Molly's side, Bobbie ventured a glance at Joe. He wasn't in uniform. None of the men were—another surprise since she had expected a full-blown Chicago PD funeral. Joe, like his brothers, wore a black wool suit, starched white shirt and black-on-black striped tie. No rank stripes, department logos or other trappings of law enforcement were visible. No coats, either. He stood a few feet apart from his siblings in unmovable solitude, the black eye patch he wore at odds with his conservative Sunday suit. His jaw clamped shut; his glacier blue eye stared at the casket. He didn't deign to give her a single blink.

No surprise there. Maybe it's for the best. If he stays away, it might make my job easier.

"May your perpetual light shine upon him," invoked the priest. "May his soul and all the souls of the faithful departed through the mercy of God rest in peace."

"Amen."

An officious undertaker toted an armful of roses. He picked single stems from the bunch, handed one to each of them and instructed them to pay their last respects. Linked to Molly and Danny, Bobbie stepped toward the casket. They placed their flowers atop the lacquered mahogany surface, stood a few moments with bowed heads and moved away from the grave to make room for others.

The brief ceremony complete, the undertaker advanced forward to the head of the casket. "There will be a luncheon reception at the home of Kay and Michael Lynch," he announced in a soft, silky voice.

"You'll come, Bobbie?" Molly's red-rimmed eyes implored her.

"Of course I will." She patted Molly's arm. "I'll meet you there."

"We have to stop at the house and pick up the kids first." Molly squeezed her hand and gave her a shy smile. "I can't wait for you to meet our little ones."

Guilt sliced through her. "I'll hardly recognize Amy. I'm sorry, Mol that—"

"Oh God, my *baby!*" Jean Sullivan's outburst shattered the stillness and pierced Bobbie's heart.

Danny strode toward his mother. Jean's living children folded around their mother to shield her from the unthinkable fact that her youngest child would be lowered into the ground forever.

Molly's body shook and Bobbie engulfed her in a hug to offer what comfort she could. Wobbly, too, she could do nothing but witness the family's suffering. They helped Jean into the car and Bobbie waited for Molly to join Danny before returning to the rental car.

****

Damn him for buying me that last beer. I never dreamed the likes of Jimmy Sullivan would hit on me at the bar. I wish I could remember. Did I really say anything about the babies? Guess I did. Somehow he knew about the Windsor Village delivery. Even though he asked for my number, I never thought he'd call. But he did. Hell, he even sprang for dinner.

Then back to his place. I knew what was going to happen and with that dreamboat I was ready. Damn him. All he wanted to do was talk about the babies.

"So how does this work? This baby racket deal you got going."

He laughed when I suggested we work on it in his bedroom. LAUGHED. No one laughs at me. But I told him all about it. Everything. Gave him the intro. Even let him take notes on his computer. Why not? He wasn't going to tell anyone. Ever.

Look at them all banded together. The high-and-mighty Sullivan family... minus one. Wish they could have seen their precious son on his knees. Wouldn't beg, though. Not like Daddy. No. Sullivan wanted to negotiate.

Maybe it didn't have to be that way with Jimmy. But he lied. They all lie to get what they want. Greedy bastard.

****

Dispirited and not up to the task before her, Bobbie drove to Kay and Mike's house. She had to park her car a block away and deal with the bone-chilling walk in the blustery January air.

She trooped into the house behind a line of other guests and entered the familiar foyer. The warmth of pleasant memories in that elegant home and the clamor of conversations around her flooded her senses.

She'd find Kay in the kitchen.

People hovered over a spread of food on the picnic-style table balancing paper plates and plastic utensils. They milled around the refrigerator and sink, Kay, a shiny blonde pixie in their midst.

"Kay, I'm so sorry." Bobbie rushed toward Jimmy's sister and threw her arms around her.

"Thank you so much for coming." Kay's voice muffled against her shoulder.

Bobbie gently released the embrace and leaned against the center island in the cheerful kitchen. The air was spiced with cinnamon and the cloying sweetness of too many carnations. Condolence bouquets covered most of the countertop space and baked goods covered the rest.

Kay sniffed and jabbed tears away from under each eye. "I've been baking, just baking. All night long. I can't seem to stop." She jerked her shoulders in a helpless shrug. "He always loved my baking. Always had a sixth sense that I was taking one of his favorites out of the oven. He would appear out of the blue..."

Kay bent at the waist with the weight of sob-wracked grief.

"Oh, honey..." Bobbie draped an arm over Kay's

shoulder.

"I called him." Mikey, Kay's eldest, stepped in front of Bobbie. Already a head taller than his mother, he had the Sullivan men's Celtic good looks and the long frame that predicted he'd have their impressive physiques as well.

Kay straightened and eyed her son. "What do you mean you called him?"

Mikey grinned at his mother. "I called all the uncles with baking alerts. Charged 'em five bucks admission, too. How do you think I bought my first bike?"

"Well, I'll be damned." Kay erupted in a bawdy, Irish barroom laugh. "You little devil."

Grateful to Mikey for finding a way to lessen his mother's pain, Bobbie joined in the laughter. They all wiped tears from their eyes when they could breathe again.

"Kay, do you know what Jimmy was working on recently?" Bobbie asked.

Kay gave her a penetrating look. "Not really. Why?"

"There may be a connection with a case I'm working on in New York."

"Really? How could that be?"

"I don't know yet. But if I can piece it together, I might be able to help find Jimmy's killer."

Kay nodded. "I wish I could help you, but as far as I know his work was routine. You should talk to Daddy and my brothers. They'll know more."

"I will." She kissed Kay on the cheek. "Thanks."

"Sure. Eat some of this food, will you? Please."

Bobbie filled a plate and wandered into the crowded den.

"Bobbie, you're a vision, young lady." John Sullivan stood up from a couch. "Jean and I are grateful you came all this way to pay your respects to our Jimmy. We've been following your career. We're very proud of you."

"Thank you, sir. That means a lot coming from you. My condolences to you both." Bobbie glanced down at the bereaved mother, seated on the loveseat.

Jean nodded, her face a mask of grief. John bent down toward his wife and squeezed her hand.

"Mr. Sullivan, do you mind answering a few questions about Jimmy's recent cases?"

"I don't mind telling you what I know, Bobbie." He gave her a wary smile. "Let's find a place to sit."

No one knew anything beyond vague generalities. The Sullivan clan was close and they made it their habit to help each other professionally when asked. Jimmy hadn't asked for help or advice based on her conversations with his dad and four out of five siblings. That left Joe.

She debated whether to question Joe or not based on the law of percentages. Why deal with him when he probably didn't know more than any of the other Sullivans?

He didn't give her a choice. A flighty shimmer of heat dove inside her. She turned as he approached. The shimmer twisted and knotted like an electric vice around her heart. In a second the welcome she intended to give him dissolved. His face was as icy as the January landscape outside.

He placed a hand around her bicep in a far from gentle grip. "Is it my turn to be interrogated?"

The physical connection jolted to her toes. The pressure of his hand, the hard line of his lips and his level stare rigid—no sign of the boyish sweetness she remembered.

"Hello, Joe." She forced a benign smile while she yanked her arm out of his hold. "I'm very sorry for your loss."

"Save it. Why are you nosing around here?"

"I'm not *nosing* around."

Angling her head to study his face, a calm descended. Her work grounded her. She was good at it and even their shared past couldn't intimidate her from doing her job. "I'm so sorry for what you must be going through. Jimmy was a wonderful person. I can only imagine—"

"Spill it, Bobbie."

She huffed in exasperation. "Whether you believe it or not, I care deeply about your family. If anything, I'm trying to help catch Jimmy's killer."

"What does a Fibbie have to do with a beat cop's death? What are you working on?"

"I'm developing a case in New York that might have Chicago ties. I think Jimmy knew something about it. Did he mention anything to you about what he was working on?"

"If he did I won't tell you, unless you tell me exactly why you want to know."

She searched his face, his eye like a polar tractor beam trained on her. She saw no warmth in that pretty blue iris rimmed in white. His eyes used to spark a sweet playfulness and look at her as if she had hung the moon. The unflinching expression on his face now was more suited to staring down a felony suspect.

She'd done nothing to earn his distrust and longed to undo whatever it was that made him look at her that way. Because she still trusted him.

"There's a connection between Jimmy and Bradley Sterling, Esquire—a New York hotshot attorney," she said. "He's the subject of the case I'm building. He's suspected of being the key player in a human trafficking ring. Babies. High-priced, private adoptions. We don't know how he gets the babies. And Jimmy talked to him. At least once."

"Bullshit."

"There are cell phone records."

"His phone was stolen."

"Really?" That knowledge elated her. "When? Did he report it?"

"Don't know. His cell is missing. And his laptop was demo'ed. They ransacked his apartment.

Nothing is left to go on."

"Well that tells us something, doesn't it? Can you get me into his apartment?" She faced him, feet planted. "Look, Joe—"

"We'll handle it here. I want you off this case."

"Not likely." She stared into his eye. "There's a connection. I just have to determine what and why."

"You think Jimmy was *dirty*?"

His tone registered like physical punishment to her. "I don't think anything. I know—."

"Forget it."

He stalked away.

She *didn't* think Jimmy was dirty, but it would do no good to follow Joe and keep hammering that home. She sighed and searched the crowded room for someone to chat with.

Everyone seemed linked in pairs. Displaced as well as aggravated, she left Kay's house as soon as she could for another dip into the refrigerated outdoors.

The cold didn't penetrate to her bones like it had before. *Downright warm out here compared to standing next to Joe.*

She slid into the car, the vinyl seats stiff and crackling beneath her, and turned on the motor. She revved it a couple times and let it idle, deep in thought.

She'd stick around for the weekend to poke around Jimmy's precinct and catch up with Molly's beautiful brood. And to think. Hard. About the Sullivans, Joe in particular.

She'd figure it all out. She always did.

****

Two days later Bobbie hugged Molly's family good-bye. Spit-up on the shoulder of her coat, she set out for O'Hare airport. Molly lived near the center of town and Bobbie had her choice of back street routes to get to the Interstate: the most direct would take her past Joe's condo complex.

With time to spare, she could take a longer route and circumvent the memory of the brutal attack in Joe's parking lot. But avoidance was never her style. She drove to the spot where a killer had slashed her and nearly made her his sixth victim.

She parked her rental car in Joe's empty parking space beneath a willow tree that loomed larger than it had more than six years ago. She let the engine idle as she recalled the event in vivid detail.

A flash of naked terror took her breath. His vileness, the brute strength of his grip had turned her into a frail rag doll. But she had used her head to buy time just like Joe had taught her. Then Joe was there. From the ground she saw his bare feet planted in the grass and his calm voice demanded that her assailant drop his weapon. A gun fired and it was over.

She inhaled a deep cleansing breath. It *was* over.

She swiveled in her seat and searched through the rear window. Joe lost his eye just over there.

And she focused on the spot where she lost Joe.

Chapter 2

Joe strained to see past the grit in his eye that burned from hours of overuse. He pinched the circuit extractor to grasp and pull charred wires from the center of a bashed piece of equipment. The thing more or less resembled a laptop computer.

Discouraged, he hit damaged keys and stared at the garbled flickers and blurs on the screen. Despite hours of painstaking work, he hadn't made much progress resurrecting the melted mess.

He stretched in his chair and rubbed his stiff neck with rough hands. His stomach growled a loud protest. Missed lunch again.

The dented metal clock on the squad room wall registered three o'clock. He had started the project at eight in the morning and still hadn't pulled much out of the piece of junk.

The key to finding Jimmy's killer had to be buried somewhere in the inner workings of his brother's computer. Hardly a coincidence that someone wanted the information destroyed. Stuck on desk duty, Joe couldn't do much to contribute to the investigation but sit there and figure out a way to extract the information somebody didn't want discovered.

He would clear his brother's name, wouldn't stop until he had all the answers. He couldn't let Roberta Leighton and her insinuations mar his brother's impeccable service record. His blood pressure soared every time she came to mind.

Her probing questions so soon after they had said their final goodbyes to Jimmy were tasteless and invasive, even if he understood on a professional level the necessity. But Jimmy's death was personal and he didn't give a rat's ass that she had a job to do. Who did she think she was? How dare she question Jimmy's ethics?

No one was more dedicated to the force than Jimmy. Joe missed his brother more each day. Jimmy had helped him move on after the attack that had cost him his career. Jimmy had convinced him, when no one else could, to go back to work, even if it was as a paper pusher. He had given Joe hope that one day he would be able to resume his normal life.

Jimmy didn't pussyfoot around him like the rest of the family. He pushed him with relentless determination to prepare for active duty. He dragged him to target practice and they worked out at the gym like they were training for an ironman triathlon. Jimmy's belief that Joe could do the improbable and be reinstated as a homicide detective almost made Joe a believer, too.

Jimmy gave him lessons on the inner workings of computers. They hung out together and became more than brothers born a decade apart. He was good-hearted and full of life. Until some bastard ended it. They were best friends and Joe missed his best friend more than he missed having two eyes.

Tired, hungry and irritated, he pulled the bottom drawer of his metal desk open and dumped the snarled mess inside with a satisfying clang. He slammed the drawer closed. Heads turned in the squad room.

"Everything all right over there, bro?"

A chair scraped on the ancient linoleum.

"Fine Brian. Just fine."

"Doesn't sound fine to me." Brian leaned his six-foot-four, taut body against the wall in front of Joe's desk. "What's wrong?"

"What's right?" Joe tugged open the drawer, dragged the twisted laptop out again and slammed it on his desk. "I've been spinning my wheels with this all day. All the information I have managed to pull off of this piece of shit is worthless."

Brian leaned over the desk and inspected the fried laptop. "I can't believe that you got any information off it at all."

"You know who could get every scrap out of this computer?"

"Who?"

"Jimmy. He was teaching me how to retrieve lost data, but nothing this complex. He could solve this. He was a miracle worker with anything mechanical."

"Tell me about it. He was the best geek I ever met. Who's going to make my DVD player stop blinking? Who am I going to call when my computer freezes? I never got the hang of technology. Poor Jimmy. I had to call him a couple times a month to set my computer straight."

Brian shook his head and averted his eyes, but not before Joe saw the tears brimming.

"I miss him, too, and you can call me anytime. I may not be able to fix all of your computer problems but I can give it a try. Jimmy taught me a lot this past year. He really was a wiz with it and a great teacher. I told him he should follow Dan to the academy, but he wouldn't give up his fieldwork. I don't blame him. Nothing would make me give it up. That is, if I still had it to give up."

"How's that coming? Anything new? Pops able to help at all?"

"No." Joe fixed an eye full of attitude on Brian's

face and gave him credit that he held the stare. He was sick of talking about his futile attempts to get back to the work he loved. He wanted his life back. He hated being chained to a desk.

"You said you didn't get any useful information out of the computer," Brian said. "What were you able to pull out of it?"

Glad for the change of subject, Joe relaxed. "I'll show you," he said as he picked a file from a pile of manila folders, precisely aligned on the corner of his desk. He straightened the pile, opened the folder and took out several sheets of paper.

"I retrieved some great family pictures. I think they're from a few Thanksgivings ago. Remember the one when Jimmy got the new camera and drove everyone, even Mom, crazy?"

"She finally took the camera away from him." Brian sat on the edge of Joe's desk, his muscular arms crossed over his chest.

"He was so mad at all of us for laughing."

"Wasn't that the same year my football team finally beat your team?"

"I don't think so. And if I remember right, I beat you with a bunch of little girls on my team." Joe handed the folder to Brian.

Brian grinned and opened it. He pulled out a photograph. "This is a great picture of Mom and Pop. I forgot Kay was pregnant with the twins that year. Look how huge she is. Can I have a copy of this for blackmail?"

Brian flipped through the file. "Mary and Amy have grown so much. They were such little girls in this picture with Bobbie. Bobbie hasn't changed at all, though. She's still hot."

The muscles in Joe's stomach tightened at the picture Brian held up. Bobbie had haunted his dreams for years and since Jimmy's funeral he had not been able to close his eyes without seeing her drawn face full of sympathy, her red hair pulled back severely from her porcelain skin. Her beautiful amber eyes bored into his soul.

"I never noticed Bobbie," Joe lied.

"You didn't notice? What is your good eye blind?"

"I don't have much use for her. She accused Jimmy of being dirty."

"No, she didn't. She asked us all a couple of questions. Jimmy's cell phone number was on that lawyer's records. Give her a break. She had to follow up. She was just doing her job."

"I won't cut her a break and I'm surprised you're siding with her."

"Calm down. I'm not siding with anyone. She didn't say that Jimmy was dirty. She hoped we'd give her information that she could use to build her case. And maybe help us find Jimmy's killer. I think you're overreacting."

Joe didn't answer him. Maybe he had overreacted, but Bobbie touched a nerve and made him furious. His anger had little to do with her questioning the family, he admitted. She showed up at his brother's funeral engaged in her successful career and didn't give a damn how that might affect him. She flaunted it in front of him. The career he wanted. The career she had taken from him. And what did he have? He had nothing but this dead-end desk job, and right or wrong he blamed her.

He didn't want to hear Brian defend her. He took a sheet of paper out of his desk drawer and waved it just out of Brian's reach.

"What do you have there?" Brian made a grab for it, but Joe had quicker reflexes and yanked it away before Brian could snatch it.

"Something that will have Kay baking and cooking for me forever. This is Aunt Theresa's secret, cheesecake recipe."

"No way. How did Jimmy get a copy? Kay's wanted it for years, but Aunt Theresa wouldn't give it to her."

"Remember? Aunt Theresa was Jimmy's godmother. She spoiled him. She must have emailed him a copy before she died."

"Yeah, but she died a couple of years ago, right? Why didn't he do anything with it?"

"Who knows? Finders keepers." Joe kissed the piece of paper with a loud smack, folded it and put it in the inside pocket of his suit jacket.

Brian beamed at him, the perfect smile that set his parents back a bundle for braces. "I want to be with you when you show it to Kay. She'll flip."

"Deal, if you help me out. I need you to check out exactly what Bobbie has so far on that lawyer."

"Why don't you just call her and ask her?"

"I'd rather not. I was pretty short with her—not exactly charming."

"You not charming? I find that hard to believe." Brian gave him a lopsided grin. "Tell me what you want to know."

"Anything she'll give you."

"I never turn down a chance to talk to a beautiful woman. I'll call her now."

Brian returned to his desk, sifted through the unholy mess of it, and came up with a business card. He sat down, glanced at the card and dialed.

He talked to Bobbie twenty minutes. Joe tried to ignore his brother's infectious laugh. Was he flirting with her? He should have called her himself.

Brian hung up the phone and Joe pounced. "What does she have?"

"Some couples' testimony how the lawyer works. Phone records. A couple Sterling burned and cancelled the adoption right about the time Jimmy was killed. Clean paper trail. She's pretty frustrated with it."

"Thanks, Brian."

"Sure."

Joe sat statue-like at his desk and mulled over a plan. It could work. All he needed was a little help.

He would be asking a lot of his father, but the proposition might appeal to Pop's instincts as a former police commissioner and he wouldn't refuse to help him.

"Hey Bri. Do you know if Mom and Pop are still at Kay's?"

"Yep. Talked to Ma this morning. She said they would be heading back to Florida tomorrow or the next day. Why?"

"Just an idea. I think I'll stop by Kay's on my way home. I want to see them before they head back and there's something I want to talk to Pop about. Want to come? I'll bring the cheesecake recipe. I bet we can score dinner with it."

"I'm there. Give me a minute to clear my desk."

If Joe could pull off his plan he wouldn't be seeing this office for a while, which suited him fine.

Chapter 3

"Have a seat, Agent Leighton." Assistant Director in Charge, Francis Monahan drew a metal chair away from the front of his government-issued, wood veneer desk and held it for her. His Old Spice aftershave was a pleasant masculine scent she'd always associated with authority.

Monahan's old-fashioned chivalry and formal address made her even more nervous than she had been when called into the top boss's sanctum. She ranked too far down to have one-on-ones with the ADIC.

He stepped behind the desk in front of a beat-up, executive-style leather chair. He had a handsome well-used face with starbursts of smile lines from each eye. Just a touch of paunch bulged above his belt. His mane of cottony white hair gave him a kind and grandfatherly appearance. Any agent who considered him benign would be sadly mistaken.

He sat, tented his hands against his chin and smiled at her. "I read your report on James Sullivan. Nice work."

"Really?" she blurted. "With all due respect, sir, there was nothing substantial in that report. A wasted trip, if you ask me...sir."

He still smiled at her.

She straightened in the chair and waited. Her back ached from tension.

"I disagree. It was a good start." He picked up the mug in front of him and took a sip. He leaned back and swiveled his chair side to side. "The connections you made with the Sullivan family laid the groundwork for the next phase of the investigation."

"Which investigation would that be, sir?"

He stared at her with his notorious intensity. That look—grim if his Irish green eyes didn't dance with inner amusement—could take a subordinate apart. Over his long career no one had ever been able to predict the man's moods.

"I'm sure I don't have to remind you about your current responsibilities, Special Agent Leighton."

"Of course not, sir." She held the stare. "However, in my estimation the Sullivan family gave me nothing to move my investigation along."

"That's about to change," he said. "I've cleared an undercover assignment I have in mind for you with your superiors. I have your written orders compiled as well as dossiers concerning the identities you'll assume as a couple." He tapped a stack of file folders on his desk.

"Yes, sir. Couple, sir?"

"You'll pose as prospective adoptive parents and infiltrate Sterling's operation. You have the rest of the day to familiarize yourself with the dossiers and take care of personal arrangements. There'll be a car at your home at seventeen hundred to take you both to the residence."

He handed her a thick folder.

"Yes, sir. Who's my partner on the operation?"

Monahan glanced over her head and beamed. He pushed his chair back and stood behind his desk. "Right on cue, Joey."

Bobbie peered over her shoulder. Joe Sullivan pushed through the door, covered the distance between him and Monahan in two strides and caught the older man up in a bear hug.

"Good to see you, Uncle Frankie," he declared in a hearty baritone.

Bobbie's mouth fell open at the good old boy display. She sucked in a breath. "Joey? Uncle Frankie?"

"It's an honorary title, Agent Leighton," Monahan said. "How's the old man, Joey?"

"He's as good as can be expected. Sends his best. He and Mom are back in Florida now."

"Sorry I couldn't make it to the funeral, son. Rose is still recuperating from surgery and can't travel yet. I hope you received the Mass card we sent."

"Thank you, we did. It meant a lot to Mom."

Bobbie stood up with enough force to topple the metal chair and faced off with the two men. "I hate to interrupt this reunion, but what the hell are you doing here, Sullivan?"

Joe put his arm around the Chief. "Don't worry, Uncle Frank. She's really happy to see me."

Joe gave her a wicked grin, a pirate who had somehow commandeered her ship. He wore khaki chinos, a Navy blue blazer and a starched shirt with a solid blue tie: a bland office uniform on anyone else.

Behind her Joe righted the chair.

Monahan chuckled. "Take a seat, Joe. Sit, Agent Leighton." He handed Joe a dossier.

She sank down and sat on the edge of her chair. All her limbs had gone wooden.

"You'll be working the Sterling case together. You'll find everything you need in that file, Joe. You'll pose as Alexander and Cynthia Baron. Alexander heads Baron Beef. Cynthia is a socialite housewife. Lots of volunteer work and such. We've set up a residence on the Upper East Side overlooking the park. It's ready for you to move in tonight for the duration of the operation."

Joe thumbed through the folder. "Okay..."

"Like hell you will," she asserted, perspiring in the suddenly over-hot room.

Apparently absorbed by the dossier balanced on the inner thigh of one leg, Joe didn't bother to acknowledge her. Even his shoe choice, scuffed cowboy boots on his huge feet, stoked her fury.

Her heart pounded in her ears. "I want to work with another field agent on this, sir. Surely, I've earned the right to have some input here..." She paused, breathing hard.

Monahan leveled his penetrating eyes on her. "Your work has been exemplary, Agent Leighton. If this operation is too much for you, I can have you reassigned to another case."

"I see." Was Sullivan actually *smirking*? She swallowed her outrage. "That won't be necessary, sir."

"Good." He switched his attention to Joe. "Any questions, Joey? Can you handle a southern drawl?"

"Suuuuure."

His sultry twang made her bite down on her tongue. Next he'd call her the little woman and she'd have to pull out her gun.

"What about clothes?" Joe piped up in a blessed Chicago flat intonation. "I packed light. Any budget to buy rich guy clothes?"

"There are wardrobes for each of you in the penthouse. 48 chest and 32 waist, right Joe? Leighton you're down as size 6."

Full of repressed frustration, she could only nod. If she offered no further resistance maybe the interview would end. And she could cold-cock Joe the minute they were out the door.

"Agent Leighton will give you her address," Monahan continued. "We've assigned a newly appointed Special Agent as your driver. He'll pick you up at seventeen hundred at Leighton's place and take you to the residence. If there's nothing more, you're free to go."

Monahan sat unblinking, an unmistakable command and absolute dismissal. She stood, Joe at her elbow and left the ADIC's office.

She didn't speak until elevators doors closed them in a downward bound car, and she had the good luck to be alone with him.

She wheeled on him. "Don't think for one minute that this is going to happen. I'll get you off this case if it's the last thing I ever do."

"Go ahead and try. You'll have to go to Washington to pull it off. Nobody has higher jurisdiction in New York than Monahan and you know it."

"How the hell is he your honorary Uncle Frankie, for the love of God?"

"He's tight with my father. Been to a lot of family things over the years."

"So you pulled strings to take over *my* case..."

The elevator opened on a lower floor and a man, identification paraphernalia swinging around his neck, entered the car.

She moved closer to Joe. "This is mine and I want you off of it," she said under her breath.

He leaned down and whispered in her ear, "You said you wanted my help at Jimmy's funeral. I'm helping."

His warm breath on the sensitive skin around her ear sent shivers through her and prickled goose bumps on her arms. She would not let him distract her. She moved away from him, mute and fuming. The floor lights blinked down in sequence. When the doors opened she charged through them.

Joe tailed her. She shoved into the ladies room and slammed into a stall. She'd sit it out in there until he disappeared. Patience wasn't a Joe Sullivan virtue.

She took out her BlackBerry and handled emails. She made several phone calls, her voice echoing hollow in the tiled lavatory. Twenty minutes later, she had caught up with her electronic correspondence and her phone messages.

She swung out of the stall, stepped to the sink and washed her hands. The simple routine calmed her. She couldn't figure a way out of the assignment, but at least she'd ditched Joe for the time being.

She pushed out the door into the hallway. She hadn't ditched Joe. Instead, she apparently had pissed him off. He slouched against the far wall with a murderous look in his eye. Much more handsome than she remembered, with that dangerous eye patch and panther-like body, ready to pounce.

"Are you *done*?" He punched the sarcasm at her.

"Yes." She turned down the hall toward her office without a backward glance, pleased that she didn't feel him follow.

"I'll take that address now," he shouted behind her.

Chapter 4

Bobbie slammed her dresser drawer shut and stomped into the closet. She tugged things off hangers and threw them over her head toward her bed. Some clothes landed on the white eyelet bedspread— some missed the mark and fell on the glossy hardwood floor.

She dragged a dusty suitcase from the back of the closet and dropped it with a thump at the foot of the queen-size bed. She knew she had a complete wardrobe waiting for her in Manhattan but she wanted--no needed--to have some familiar things with her while she lived the life of the fictional Cynthia Baron.

She folded lingerie and tucked it into the case. Several silk blouses, ultra-short skirts and tight pants might do for the arm-candy wife of a cattleman. She packed with calm efficiency while her mind screamed in silent frustration. *I can't believe I have no say in my own case.*

Nothing she'd done since she left the field office that morning to banish aggravation had worked. She had scrubbed her apartment's floors and walls until her hands were abraded and her joints ached. Normally, the fresh pine scent and gleaming surfaces after a few hours of rigorous cleaning filled her with accomplishment and contentment in her surroundings. Instead, the manual labor stoked her annoyance.

Furious with Joe, the vein in her neck pulsed. How dare he snake his way into her job? Her investigation? Her life? He was so smug with his "Uncle Frankie."

The good old boy network! She had been fighting it from the first day she entered the Academy. She had to be quicker, stronger, and smarter than her male counterparts. She had worked, worried and fought her way to her current position at the FBI. Until Joseph Sullivan strolled into her work place, she was proud of her accomplishments and hard-won reputation.

There hadn't been an *Uncle Frankie* to pave the way for her. Not that it mattered. She would never stoop to take advantage of connections. If she did, she would be labeled a user.

He's not labeled a user. No, he's a clever male who knows how to work the system. And I'm a second-class female who has to accept his manipulations or be taken off my own case.

She threw a wooden hanger across the room. It dinged the spotless wall.

"Damn it!"

Her front door opened and closed.

"Darling? Did you just curse at me?"

I don't need this right now. She took a deep breath. "No, David. I cursed at a hanger," she called. "I'll be right there. I have to leave in a few minutes. I don't want to be late."

She frowned at her reflection in the dresser mirror. Her ripped, gray Bears sweatshirt fell off her shoulder and strands of hair escaped in auburn tendrils out of the rubber band on top of her head. She sawed at the smudged mascara under her eyes with her finger.

David came into her bedroom and halted, his face contorted like he smelled rotten eggs.

"You're right, Roberta. We don't want to be late." He surveyed the room. His face pinched deeper and she forced down a shimmer of revulsion at his unattractive expression.

"I really don't have time. The car's going to be here in a half hour," she said.

"It doesn't sound like you're talking about our dinner date with Father tonight."

Most days it just annoyed her when he called her dad, father, as if he staked a claim to him, and by inference, to her. After a day of mounting irritations, his reference to Dad incensed her.

But guilt tinged her anger since she had completely forgotten the dinner date. She didn't have the heart to confront him.

"I'm sorry, David. I have to work. Can you give me a minute to finish up here? I'll explain."

"I suppose." He walked away.

His sullen movements distanced her further from the man she'd dated exclusively for two years. Her father, impressed with David's work experience and his cum laude degree from Yale, had recruited him to work at the firm. His Ivy League diploma meant more to Dad than all her accomplishments put together.

When she was assigned to the field office in New York, Dad had hatched his plan and arranged a lavish dinner at Tavern on the Green to engineer her blind date with David. They had been together ever since. She supposed her willingness to accept her father's matchmaking had a lot to do with their confusing history.

Her mother died when she was four. Her father had pushed her away as if punishing her for the death of the love of his life. She grew and so did his estrangement from her. That made her feel rejected and guilty for something she couldn't name. When she was old enough to understand that she had nothing to do with the leukemia that took her mother way too young, it was too late to mend the father-daughter relationship.

Nothing Bobbie ever did was good enough for her father. If she received an A, where was the A plus? When she finished second in her high school class, he was disappointed she wasn't first. She spent most of her life trying to please him.

Five years ago, she pleased herself and had joined the FBI without his blessing. Two years ago, she finally earned her father's approval. She had finished first in her class in the Academy and was the youngest female Special Agent to receive the Director and President's commendations. That should have gained her the nod from Dad. None of the accomplishments that meant so much to her had earned his esteem. Her relationship with David Harper won her father's long awaited blessing.

Bobbie liked David's directness, respected his intelligence and his obvious infatuation flattered her. She was comfortable with him. And had grown fond of him, although she refused to discuss marriage despite how frequently he brought up the subject. The hand-picked son and business heir-apparent her father never had, Dad fully expected her to marry the man and make it official.

Not yet. She wasn't sure that she loved David.

He loomed in front of her doorway again. "I'm waiting, Roberta."

Faced with his unyielding impatience, it was hard to feel anything for him but dull resignation.

"I don't want to fight about this. I have no choice. I have an assignment that starts tonight."

"Did you at least try to get out of it? Didn't you tell them that you had plans for this evening? Important plans. Father wants us to schmooze the Bromley's. Tony Bromley sits on three corporate boards and he could sway a lot of business our way."

"I really am sorry, okay? I know this dinner is important to you." She snapped her valise shut. "I would go if I could, you know that. But I can't."

Honestly, David or dinner plans never entered her mind all day. Another pang of guilt pinched her.

"This is unacceptable," he groused. "Father will be very disappointed with you again."

She hated when he talked to her in that flat, schoolmaster tone and made her feel like a tardy schoolgirl. Sometimes the ten-year difference in their ages was too wide a gap to bridge. Plus, "Father" wasn't his parent.

"*My* father will just have to accept that my job is more important than any dinner with a client. Lives are at stake with my work."

She met his eyes and read the opposition in his pale blue glare. Dismay curled inside her because he didn't understand her, and probably never would.

"Please spare me the saving society speech, Roberta." His voice quivered. "Can you just come and make a quick appearance? You can grab a cab and be back in an hour or two."

He wheedled her because he was afraid to face her father alone when she was expected to be there, too, but she couldn't do more than try to placate him. "I don't have time. I have to change my clothes before the car gets here. As you said, Dad is used to being disappointed in me. I'll call him and smooth things out for you, okay?"

"All right. Thanks." His expression tired and dejected. "Where are you going? How long will you be gone? I'll miss you."

He meant well. He had told her many times that he loved her. She refused to lie to him and hadn't reciprocated. But she cared for him and would never willfully hurt him.

A surge of tenderness had her sliding her arms around his waist. She hugged the familiar softness, angled her head down and nuzzled his neck. He smelled of Old Spice aftershave, just like her father.

"Please don't be mad at me. I can't tell you where or how long I'll be undercover. You know I would rather be with you."

"I'm not sure of anything anymore." His arms encircled her waist. "Ever since you came back from Chicago you've been acting different."

She raised her head off his shoulder. "It's this case. I can't get it out of my mind. I have to find the answers. I promise as soon as it's over everything will be back to normal."

She leaned toward him for a kiss and closed her eyes when their lips met. Joe's face flashed in her mind. A lazy smile played at the corners of his lips, dimpling his cheeks. The sapphire gleam in his eye taunted and dared. Alarmed, she snapped her eyes open to expel the vision.

Her lips stayed connected with David's, but her memories tumbled, disjointed. Were there no limits to Joe's tampering with her life? How had she let him invade her private moments? She was supposed to love David.

She teetered when David ended the kiss.

Yes, I'm supposed to love David. She tugged him towards the clothes strewn bed. She needed him to blot out Joe's presence in her bedroom.

"We can't, Roberta." Desire glazed his eyes. Yet he held her at arm's length.

"Of course we can. Why can't we?"

"For one thing, Father is waiting."

"Let him wait." She unbuttoned his shirt but his fingers followed hers, fastening what she undid.

He clasped her hands and gave her a playful grin. "I thought you were in a hurry to go to work."

"Work can wait, too." Her hands dove toward his shirt buttons again.

His hesitation froze her frenzied fingers. "I want you, David. Don't you want me?"

"You know I do. But I have a weird feeling

something else is going on with you. What is it?"

"Nothing. I have no idea what you mean. I don't know how long we'll be apart. That's all."

He stepped back. His ardent stare unnerved her. *What is wrong with me?*

The doorbell chimed like the round had ended.

"The car's early," she said, glad for the interruption.

"Finish up in here. I'll get it."

She followed him out of the room so she could give instructions to the driver herself. He reached the door first.

Joe Sullivan filled the doorway. All the air seemed to be sucked out of her home and she had difficulty catching her breath. Joe leaned against the door molding. A weathered Stetson shadowed his face and dimmed the wattage of the glint in his eye. He wore a blue tweed blazer over snug denim jeans. The first few buttons of his white oxford shirt were unbuttoned. A replay spooled in her head of her fingers working open the remaining buttons on Joe's shirt instead of David's.

She blinked it away and positioned herself at David's side. She caught a musky whiff of Joe's cologne. She ignored its earthy scent and the pleasure-tug it invoked.

Pent-up fury coiled inside her again and she snapped, "What are you doing here?"

"Howdy, ma'am," he drawled with perfect Lone Star pitch. He touched the brim of his hat with maddening virility. "You don't sound glad to see me, little lady."

David stood mute next to her.

"Knock off the cowboy act, Joe," Bobbie demanded. "We're not on duty yet. I asked what you're doing here?"

Chapter 5

Joe noticed her torn sweatshirt and trained his eye a few seconds on the pale cream skin of her exposed shoulder. No evidence of bra straps prompted musing about the rest of the skin beneath threadbare material. *Damn she looks good.*

"Are you just going to stand there and stare?" she demanded.

He raised his eye to the level of her face. "As Monahan said, we begin the assignment tonight from here. Your rookie Fibbie is double-parked in front of your building, shaking like a leaf that he'll get a ticket."

Joe chuckled and brushed past Bobbie into her apartment. "Doesn't look like the kid has ever been undercover before. He's all impressed that he gets to drive *the* Special Agent Leighton around."

Bobbie stared at him like he had uttered Swahili.

He cocked an eyebrow and laid thick the Texas drawl, "Did you forget about tonight, lil' darlin'?"

"Don't darlin' me. How could I forget how you used your Uncle Frankie to worm your way in to my investigation?" Her crystalline-honey eyes pierced him like she aimed to cut him in two. If a look were enough, he'd already be dead.

"Let's get something straight." He threw some indignation back at her. "It's not your investigation. It's our investigation. I have as much right to be in this as you. Maybe more. Because of my brother."

"I'm sorry." She didn't look it. "I must have missed the announcement. Exactly when did you become an FBI agent?"

The short, little guy next to her cleared his throat and broke Joe's concentration.

"Would somebody please tell me what's going on here? Who the hell is Uncle Frankie? And who the hell are you?" He frowned at Bobbie and glared up at Joe.

Joe offered his hand toward him, "I'm—"

"Shut up, Joe," Bobbie interrupted. "He's Detective Joseph Sullivan. Homicide. Chicago. Joe, this is David Harper."

She huffed a sigh and the sweatshirt material dipped lower off her shoulder. "I have to change. Joe, have a seat or something. David was just about to leave."

She spun and stalked away from them. Both watched her retreat. David caught Joe check out her hip action and squinted at him in disapproval.

Joe regarded him evenly. "I don't want to hold you up. Nice to meet you, Dave."

He held out his hand again and Dave shook it.

"Actually, it's David, Joseph. I'm not in that big a rush. Can I get you something to drink?"

The standoff continued while the pressure each man exerted on the handclasp increased with each downturn of the shake.

"Actually, it's Joe, Dave. A beer would hit the spot if you have it."

Joe broke the handhold and turned toward a seating area. He settled on the oversized, cushiony sofa. He plucked off his hat by its crown and set it down on the glass-topped, coffee table.

Painted in warm earthy tones, shades of pale peach to deep brick created a homey feel. The room had a definite female touch minus the frills. Neat, uncluttered, it appealed to him.

He glanced at the gleaming granite counter that separated the living area from the kitchen where David opened the fridge. He seemed at home. Did they live together? The thought of her living with David made his muscles clench.

He squelched the urge to be nasty to David. What did he care what she did in her personal life?

David handed him an iced pilsner glass and took a seat in the small, black leather recliner on the other side of the coffee table. It could be "his" chair. Joe pushed down another urge to bait the guy.

"Thanks, David. I'm drinking alone?"

"I have an engagement. So how long have you and Roberta been working together? I don't think she has ever mentioned you. Your name seems familiar, though."

"We knew each other back in Chicago when she worked for my sister-in-law. We were given the assignment today. This is our first case. How long have you two been together? She never mentioned she had a boyfriend."

"A bit more than a boyfriend," he asserted, his tone arrogant. "We've been together two years and plan to marry."

"Really?" Joe sized him up. Too old for her, he figured. Dishonest, too, judging from the body language.

"Congratulations. What do you do?"

"Investment banking. I work at Roberta's firm."

"Bobbie has a firm?"

"Yes. Well, it's hers in name only. Her mother left it to her, but her father runs the company. I work for him."

"Interesting." Joe sipped the beer, pleased that his silence seemed to make David nervous.

The click of high heels and the scuff of something dragged along the floor broke the silence.

"I'm almost ready." Bobbie appeared, bent unevenly from towing a bulky suitcase behind her.

Joe jumped up to help her with the bag but the sight of her froze him in place.

She turned to David. "Did you see my purse anywhere?"

"I hung it on the bathroom doorknob. I found it on the floor again."

"Thanks."

They stared at her, dead quiet.

"What?" She let go of the suitcase and inspected herself. "Is my slip showing? Can't be... I'm not wearing one."

She looked amazing, her hair piled on top of her head in a mass of crazy curls, caught in a diamond clip. A skintight, electric blue dress hugged every curve down to mid-thigh where about a mile of leg perched in wet dream stilettos. Her eyes, framed with smudges of gray, an invitation for a man to heat-smoke into flame.

She is beautiful. What have I done? How can I live with her and not touch her?

"You look incredible." David beat him to the simple truth.

"Yes," Joe said.

"Thanks," she said.

A little distance from her wouldn't hurt. Plus, he wanted to ditch the eye patch. "Mind if I use your bathroom for a minute?" Joe asked.

"Yeah, sure." Bobbie pointed behind her. "Down the hall on your right."

Joe passed by her and a blast of flowery scent hit him. Gardenias. They had always been his flower of choice when he thought about such things in the past. It had been a long time since he breathed in their heady fragrance.

He closed himself in her bathroom and took a

packet and some tape out of his jacket pocket. The room smelled like pine, dainty and pristine—spotless, too. He could see his blurred face reflected in the white porcelain sink.

He stared in the mirror over the sink, removed his black eye patch and stuffed it in his jacket pocket. He ripped the packet open and held a square patch of gauze over the half-moon scar tissue where his left eye once had been. He tore off pieces of adhesive tape and secured the gauze around its perimeter.

Satisfied, he stuffed the scraps of paper wrap into his other pocket and opened the door. He took her purse off the knob on the other side and hooked it over his forearm on his way to the living room.

"Here you go." He handed her the purse.

"Thanks." She searched his face.

"A little LASIK surgery gone bad," he drawled.

She nodded and turned toward her befuddled fiancé. She leaned down and kissed David's cheek. "I don't know when I will be able to call. I'm sorry about missing dinner."

She made a move toward the suitcase, but Joe hefted it up in one hand.

She shook her head, flounced her tangle of red, spiral curls and took on her new persona.

The transformation was awesome.

"Okay, Daddy, are you ready to go?" Her twang stretched each word like honey sliding slow off a spoon.

He picked his hat off the coffee table and put it on. "Yes, Cici darlin', I believe I am."

Cattleman Alexander "Daddy" Baron offered his trophy wife, Cici, his arm. She placed a warm, delicate hand over his bicep like a possessive wife would.

David winced and she pulled her hand away. "It's the case," she said in a rush, sounding every bit the New Yorker. "We'll wrap it up as soon as we can.

I promise I'll be in touch."

She kissed David's cheek again and left the apartment, pure entertainment on high heels that neither man missed.

Joe tipped his hat. "Thanks for the beer, Dave. I'll take good care of her." He moved toward the door.

Bobbie appeared, framed in the doorway, and he almost collided with her. Her hair was a fiery halo and her eyes shot almond flames towards him.

"Did I hear you say you'll *take care* of me?"

He had never been faced with a more apt living definition of spitting mad before.

"Calm down." He smiled to humor her and laughed when the simple statement inspired criminal intent in her eyes.

Joe glanced over his shoulder at David. "Change of words, Dave, my friend. I'll take her off your hands."

She pursed her lips and then swiveled on those mighty fine heels to dismiss him. He followed her to the only way out of the building, not because she wanted him to do her unspoken bidding.

They rode the elevator without speaking—fine with him. She had the right to be fighting mad. Hell, he was pissed, too. He had been so driven to get out from behind the desk that he hadn't anticipated the crazy scheme his father and Monahan would concoct.

She steamed outside and pointed to the trunk of the double-parked sedan.

"Put my suitcase in the trunk," she ordered and then shoved into the back seat of the car.

"Yes, ma'am." He heaved the suitcase in and slammed down the hood.

A quick look inside told him she had no intention of sliding over on the seat to accommodate him. He rounded the car and inched into the back on the traffic side.

"What do you have in that thing, rocks?"

"A few things. Books. Not that it's any of your business."

She stared straight ahead, her delicate profile set like alabaster.

"Ready, ma'am?" The kid in the front turned back toward Bobbie, his face eager and glowing with hero worship.

"Yes, Agent Donaldson. I'm ready."

He glanced at Joe. "And are you ready, Joe?"

She leaned forward and touched Donaldson's shoulder. "Let's get a few things straight first. Detective Sullivan is, 'sir', to you, Donaldson. He holds several Medals of Valor for his work in homicide."

"Begging your pardon, sir..."

"Ah, well..." Joe said.

"But," Bobbie's voice rang like a drill sergeant, "as of now, and for the duration of this operation, we are Mr. and Mrs. Baron, Donaldson."

"Yes, ma'am...um...Mrs. Baron."

"What's your first name, Donaldson?" She toned the pitch down to conversational.

"John. It's John."

"Thank you, John. We'd like to go home, please." The Texas rose bloomed in every word.

John turned forward and merged the car with laudable courage into the tangle of slow moving traffic.

Joe's senses were saturated with gardenia fragrance and the heat of Bobbie's nearness. His discomfort about heading towards a shack-up with a belligerent federal agent who smelled that good and looked that great expanded in his chest like rising dough.

If she were a stranger he could manage. A pretty face and alluring body had never diverted him during an investigation. He could partner with anyone male or female. But Bobbie?

When he met her years ago, she had him

39

believing in love at first sight. He stared out the window of the car and smiled at the memory of her using a move he had taught her in a self-defense class that resulted in breaking a nose. In this particular instance, his. She was a blend of pure guts and modest sweetness then. And fun, too. She had taken superb care of his niece, Amy, and his sister-in-law, Molly. Bobbie loved intensely and for a while she had beamed some of that intensity at him.

The car sped past Trump-style real estate and he focused on what lay ahead. He would partner with Bobbie in this strange illusion, but the past would dog him. He had cared for her until he had saved her life.

And lost his.

Chapter 6

"Okay, guys, show time." Bobbie's stomach clenched with a jolt of adrenaline.

The car slowed and Donaldson steered to the curb in front of the stately high-rise. Clots of dingy February snow dotted the paths and shaded areas of Central Park across the street, but the sidewalk that stretched in front of the stone and brick residences was immaculate. Snow didn't dare stick to the shoes of the elite with old money in their pockets.

She swiveled and stretched both her legs out the open car door, planted her skinny high heels on the pavement and accepted the gloved hand of the doorman with calculated grace.

"Why, thank you kindly," she purred.

She stepped up the curb, clasped her hands in front of her and surveyed her surroundings up, down, around, like an ecstatic child with a stack of presents before her. She breathed in the rarified air of the Upper East Side and smiled at the doorman like she was the happiest woman on earth.

"I'm Cici Baron." She held out her hand to the uniformed black man.

He smiled and clasped it. "Pleased to meet you, Mrs. Baron. I'm Clarence."

"Clarence, such a distinguished name." She glanced at Joe who unfurled his long body from the car.

"Daddy, this is Clarence," she trilled. "Clarence, my husband, Alexander."

She shivered in her skimpy dress. Joe took his jacket off, draped it around her shoulders and touched the brim of his hat with a lazy smile in Clarence's direction. Pleased that Joe kept his mouth shut, she took the lead.

"Clarence, can you be a dear and help John with our bags?" She hooked her arm around Joe's, patted his bicep and hated her "wifely" sense of possessiveness. "C'mon, Daddy. I just can't *wait* to see our little penthouse, can you?"

Donaldson rounded the car and dug in the trunk for their bags. She turned her back on him and nudged Joe to walk along with her. Clarence rushed to beat them to the door before they stepped inside the marble-clad foyer.

Huge, bronze floor urns, burnished table pots and ornate vases arranged with fresh flowers adorned the lobby and the air smelled like a florist's shop. They waltzed into the elevator, held open by a smiling attendant.

Her head spun on the upward ride, her stomach hollow and her body feverish with Joe so near. She couldn't decide if attraction or anger fired through her.

Pretend he's Alexander and immerse in the undercover op, then maybe it wouldn't matter.

It did.

She promised herself she'd be practical. She wanted to take down Sterling and if she had to deal with Joe to do that, she'd have to make the best of it.

They entered the apartment through a long, mahogany paneled hallway. Gilt framed art, original to Bobbie's cultured eye, hung at intervals. Probably agency-seized contraband.

The foyer emptied into a yawning space divided by rectangles of Persian carpet topped with Hepplewhite and Victorian furniture groupings. Two crystal chandeliers that dangled sixteen feet above her cast muted light on polished surfaces. The satin finished wood floors edged the rugs like black cherry frames.

Joe stood, his back to her, with his legs in a wide vee, the front of his body visible in blurred reflection off a solid glass wall. She stalked in front of him and closed the heavy damask drapes.

His wonderstruck expression wouldn't do.

"Don't gawk. You're used to all this, remember?" She brushed past him and roamed through a tributary hallway off the dining area. She passed the butler's pantry, where a wine refrigerator emitted a low electronic hum, and entered the kitchen.

Gleaming copper pots hung on iron hooks over a butterscotch, granite-topped island. A restaurant quality stove with heavy grates hulked in one corner and a wall-sized refrigerator partially hid among the dark cherry cabinetry. Yards of taupe granite counters angled the room's perimeter and forty cabinets of various sizes housed who knew what in the latest kitchen tableware and gadgetry.

The room temperature changed as Joe came up behind her.

"I'm going to *love* cooking in this kitchen." She smiled and turned toward him into a soft collision with his chest. The contact lasted seconds but evoked sweet memories of months with Joe. She stepped away from his tantalizing warmth and somehow resisted jumping back, scalded by the expression on his face, dark, intense, almost a scowl.

"You'll be in charge of meals then," he grunted.

She frowned. "My meals, yes. Cook for yourself or starve...Daddy."

The doorbell chimed—a snobby classical riff, of course, not a commoner's ding-dong.

"Jesus." His eye widened and rolled sideways. "This place gives me the creeps."

She laughed despite her discomfort with him. "To the manor born." She hurried to the door.

"Oh, Clarence, honey. Just come on in." She led the way through the hall and chattered. "The movers did such a good job, didn't they, Clarence?"

"Yes, ma'am."

"Every little thing seems right in place to me."

In the dining/living room area, Joe squatted in front of the fireplace and lit kindling with a long, wooden match. Right in role based on all those fictional campfires Alexander must have lit beneath the Texas sky on cattle drives.

"Just put those down right here," she responded in answer to the questioning look in the doorman's eyes. "Daddy will put them where they belong later, won't you, Daddy?"

She regarded Joe with as much adoration as she could muster.

"No problem, darlin."

The kindling took the match and the fire licked higher along the logs. Joe stood up, pinched the brim of his hat and plopped it on a coffee table. He reached an arm behind his body and pulled out his wallet. The motion drew her attention to his slim hips. He sauntered toward Clarence with a slightly bow-legged cowboy gait that was sexy as hell. He held a fifty-dollar bill toward the doorman.

"No sir." Clarence backed away from Joe. "My pleasure to help you settle in. Have a nice evening."

He left the room. The door latch clicked shut with a discreet metallic pop.

"Good thing." Joe stuffed the bill back in his wallet and tossed it down on the table. "This is my last fifty bucks."

They were alone with no further expected interruptions. Bobbie and Joe stood in the opulent apartment and stared at each other. The fire crackled and danced shadows along the hearth. His cropped black hair mashed around his face from the Stetson. The gauze over his eye instead of the patch made him look injured instead of roguish. Vulnerable and boyish, like he once had. Maybe she wasn't so mad at him after all.

"We have work to do." His blunt tone and the glacial look in his eye snapped her back to reality.

"Right." She slipped his jacket off her shoulders and held it out toward him draped over her fingertips at the end of an outstretched arm. He took it from her and she turned away. She grabbed the handle of her suitcase and heaved it behind her down an unexplored hallway, passing a bathroom and study, through double-doors into the master— and only—bedroom.

She tugged her suitcase next to the canopied bed. Although king sized and high enough that she'd need the little steps that poked from under the lace-fringed skirt to climb in, the bed still dwarfed the huge space.

The lovely room suited her taste. The pastel walls and luxurious bed linens soothed her frayed nerves. She placed both hands on the mattress, pushed up off the floor and vaulted into the center of the bed. She splayed her arms and legs over the silky material and stared up at the crocheted canopy. Her stomach growled. The muted gabble of a television announcer reminded her that she had an unwelcome housemate in the next room.

What to do about sleeping arrangements?

She slid off the bed and sat cross-legged on the floor, pulling her suitcase toward her. She rummaged in the briefcase she had tossed inside earlier hoping she'd find a forgotten protein bar in there somewhere and came up empty. Standing, she placed the dossier Monahan had given her on the bedside table.

She unpacked her things. Finished, she kicked

her shoes into the room-sized closet and contorted her arms behind her to pull down the zipper on her dress. She shimmied out of the clingy garment, unbuckled the holster around her upper thigh and put the .22 caliber handgun in the bedside table drawer. She stripped off her panty hose.

"Question..."

She spun toward the door at the sound of his voice. Virtually naked in her bra and panties, she'd be damned if she'd show her self-consciousness.

He wore his eye patch again. He appraised her as if she was edible and he was very, very hungry.

"Mustard or mayo?"

"What?" She blurted, horrified.

"There's sandwich stuff in the fridge. Do you like mustard or mayo on a club sandwich?"

"Don't you knock?" She wanted to wipe that half smile off his gorgeous face.

"Okay." He rapped his knuckles on a door panel. "The door was open. Do you want a sandwich or not?"

Her skin flamed. The trail of blushes making a slow burn across both cheeks, down her neck and across her cleavage, had to be visible. She forced her shoulders to relax and her legs to be still, instead of beating a retreat into the closet.

"Sure. Mustard. I'll be right out."

He didn't act on her dismissal right away. Instead, his steady concentration on her body made her skin prickle.

God I want a robe. Paralyzed in the standoff she was about to grab anything to cover up when he left the room.

She held her hand to her chest and breathed, slow and steady. In the closet she grabbed a soft robe off a hanger. She tied the robe closed around her waist then took it off and hung it up again. She wanted more armor between her and that hungry stare of his. She slipped into sweats and a T-shirt, grabbed the dossier and ventured out into the main living area.

Joe propped his long legs on the coffee table, the knotted muscle of one calf leaning on its edge. His feet, crossed at the ankle, about two feet high in his socks. A napkin spread open in his lap he had half a thick sandwich in one hand and a can of beer in the other. He took a huge bite of bread, followed it with a swig from the can and stared up at a fifty-inch plasma screen hung above the fireplace mantle.

A clone of his sandwich, cut evenly in two, sat on a plate on the coffee table. He had placed a folded napkin to the right of the plate and an unopened can of beer to its left. The simple, kind gesture made her heart swell.

"That looks so good." She sat down next to him on the narrow settee, picked up a sandwich half and took a generous bite.

"Ummm," she said with her mouth full. "Starved."

She polished off half the meal in minutes, reached for the other half and settled back against the stiff backrest. "What are you watching?"

"Cable."

She looked up at the screen. Brad Pitt and Angelina Jolie sat in a formal dining room picking at their dinners and making inane small talk.

"Mr. & Mrs. Smith?" She snorted. "Perfect. There must be a machine gun in a hidden compartment around here somewhere."

"A machine gun? Here? Where?"

"You haven't seen this movie?"

"No."

"You'll see." She drained her beer and noticed his empty next to his plate. "Want another beer?"

"Sure."

"Was it in the fridge?"

"Is now. I brought a six pack with me."

"Okay." She went for two beers and tossed one to

him underhand.

She sat next to him, reaching for the dossier. She sipped her beer while methodically reading each page.

A third of the way through the thick folder, she found the medical records section for the Baron couple. She read her invasion of privacy first. It appeared that the records were actually hers, minus her real name and social security number.

She turned the page and focused on Alexander's records, finding documentation for the so-called LASIK surgery problem and a subsequent corrective surgery. She skimmed a lab results page.

"What the hell?" Bobbie reread the entry twice before she threw her head back and belly laughed.

"You're shooting blanks, Daddy dear." She laughed so hard it gave her a case of the hiccups. Tears streamed down her face.

"What are you talking about?" He angled his head toward her with the look of a semi-tolerant parent.

"Almost non-existent sperm count, Alex." She handed him the lab report. "Shooting blanks."

She could hardly contain the glee as he read the sheet. He tossed it back over toward the open folder in her lap without looking at her. "I'm not shooting blanks."

"Oh, yes, you are. But you're adoring Cici won't hold it against you." She laughed again. And hiccupped again. "I feel so much better now."

She held her breath and counted to fifteen to banish the hiccups. She let the breath out with a satisfied whoosh.

He clicked off the TV. "We should get some sleep."

"Okay. I'll rinse these dishes before I go to bed since you made the meal."

She stacked the plates and balanced the empty cans on top.

He stood up. "I'll go in there and use the bathroom first," he said.

The plates crashed on the table so fast that the two beer cans clattered to the floor. She laid her hand flat on his chest. The muscles beneath his cotton shirt were ridged and warm to the touch. A distraction if she allowed it to be.

"You better not mean the master bathroom. Because that room's off limits."

"Where am I supposed to sleep?"

"Not my problem. You wanted in to my case, you figure it out."

"Bed's big enough," he said looking at her evenly.

"I didn't think you were looking at the bed."

"I did, briefly."

Her pulse sped up but she held his stare calmly. "I'm not sharing a bed with you."

"Wouldn't matter if we did. We don't even like each other."

"That's not..." She swallowed the word *true*. "Relevant."

She picked up the dishes, collected the stray cans and took them into the kitchen. She couldn't stop him if he ignored her demands, unless she put a bullet in him. Tempting. But she hoped unnecessary. She gambled that his code of honor wouldn't allow him to invade a lady's bedroom.

When she returned, he stood in the middle of the living room with a blanket over one arm and a pillow in his hand. He eyed the narrow settee and other furniture in the room like he measured them for size. Nothing there would fit that six-foot-four frame no matter how long he stared at it.

"Maybe we could buy an air mattress or futon tomorrow," she conceded.

"I'll manage." He didn't look at her.

Guilty, but not enough to share or give up her bed that night, she lied, "I'll take the bedroom for a week. Then you. We'll alternate."

She'd renegotiate when her week was up.

"Fine. Good night. And you're welcome for dinner." His neutral expression intensified her guilt.

"Yes, thanks, Joe. It was very good. Good night."

She closed the bedroom door leaving it unlocked. He wouldn't follow her, but a fleeting sensation deep within aroused hopes he might.

She fell into bed and dreamed about the man on the other side of her door.

****

The floor proved to be more comfortable than the stick furniture. Joe had camped outside plenty with his brothers when they were kids, even in the backyard on summer nights under Jean and John Sullivan's watchful eyes. A hard bed never fazed him then.

But that was decades ago and his body protested when he rolled off the scrap of carpet that had served as his mattress and stood with a grunt to face the day.

The grit in his eye didn't help his black mood. It didn't help that she ran the shower water either. His body yearned to stand under a hot spray to ease the knots in his muscles. But not before using them to pin Bobbie to the shower wall and ravish her until they both ached all over.

He wanted her. He couldn't blame his mood on just the lack of a soft bed beneath him. He had always wanted her even when he had pushed her away for good. The women in his family had hounded him to stop her from leaving Chicago. He hadn't listened. Most of the years since then, he hadn't regretted his decision to turn his back on what they had before he lost his eye. But there were times, especially during the vulnerable nights, when he longed to let himself feel again. Last night qualified in spades.

She sang in the shower. Her voice was muffled

by distance and closed doors, but the melody was clear enough for him to know she wasn't concerned if he still slept. What a brat. He smiled anyway. There was only one Bobbie.

The sound of running water was replaced by the whine of a blow drier. He stretched, ambled toward the windows and opened the drapes. Thin streaks of sun outlining the blanket of low clouds didn't do much to brighten the dull gray day. The park was colorless with stripped trees and brown lumps of snow. But the view was awesome despite the cheerless weather. He stood mesmerized. Privileged to be there, he liked working again, in topnotch surroundings, with her.

They'd meet Sterling today. They'd be grilled and he was prepared. He had memorized the dossier before he stretched out on the floor with the thin blanket tucked around him. He knew Bobbie had memorized it, too. Both folders would be shredded before they left the apartment.

He was up for whatever this interview held. Holding back on turning the tables and interrogating the lawyer would take every ounce of discipline. Did Bradley Sterling murder Jimmy? Joe wasn't sure. When he was, he'd need all his strength not to kill in vengeance.

"Mornin', Daddy. Isn't this the most heavenly day?"

Ah, the sweet sound of his little yellow rose's voice. Like a jackhammer on stubborn concrete. He turned. She dressed in character. The pink suit of stretchy knit material she wore could be labeled conservative if it wasn't so tight and there were six inches more skirt. She wore a heavy strand of pearls that dipped into her cleavage and made a man wish he were a necklace.

"Heavenly," he agreed, pure sarcasm.

"You best get showered or we'll be late for our adoption interview, sweetie." She beamed at him, bright-eyed, eager and phony as her southern accent.

"I have time." He turned back toward the window away from the confused feelings of lust and fury she stoked in him.

She came up behind him and stood at his side. "It's amazing, isn't it?" Texas twang absent for the moment.

He nodded.

"I almost forgot how much I enjoyed just looking out a window here. Better than watching television."

"You were on assignment here before?"

"No. I used to live in this building."

"You're shitting me. When was this?"

"When I was little. With my mother..." Her hooded eyes trained straight ahead. "And for several years after she died. We moved to Park Avenue after that. Dad still lives there."

"Dave said something about *your* firm. What's that all about?"

"Nothing." She folded her arms under her breasts. He did like looking at her breasts. "Go get showered, Joe."

****

The stinging, hot shower spray worked wonders. He drew a dense, Turkish towel off the hook and wrapped it around his waist. After he smeared a steam-free circle on the mirror at eye level, he surveyed his face.

His disfigured eyelid always made him pause as if he didn't recognize his own reflection. With Bobbie in the next room the daily wave of bitterness packed an extra jolt.

He shaved then reapplied a bandage over the constant reminder that he was less than what he should be.

The doorbell chimed. *Who's that?* He put on his clothes and ventured out into the living room to find out.

Bobbie's jacket hung open, her chin inches from the crown of a man who crouched in front of her, taping a wire in place on her torso. The black thread of the device—ugly and sinister, marring her creamy skin—was placed near the tender swell of her breasts under the dainty lace bra.

Her eyes locked on him. He understood the flash of vulnerability and longing he saw in those honey-colored depths. In a split second her wistful look disappeared.

"You're next, Sullivan," she commanded.

The technician stood up. She clutched the flaps of her jacket closed while she fastened the buttons.

Joe took off his suit jacket and tie and tossed them over the back of a chair. He hitched his shirt flaps out of his trousers and undid the buttons.

"I'll wear the wire. You don't have to," he said.

"He might separate us."

He nodded and stood passive while the techie attached the wire to his chest.

Her eyes never left his over the technician's head.

Chapter 7

Donaldson maneuvered the stretch limo through the bumper-to-bumper traffic like a New York cabdriver. Bobbie admired his sure movements from the soft leather cocoon of the back seat.

Donaldson might be a rookie, but she knew the caliber of his training. She had faith in that skill and would have given a lot if a fellow agent could work the UC operation with her. Instead she was lead UC agent for the first time and her partner was a rusty cop who hated her. She'd be happier if Donaldson sat back there in the Baron's privileged world with her and Joe chauffeured them around. She would be a lot happier with her Glock on her, too, but she'd never get through security screening at Sterling's building.

She had to forget how naked the lack of her weapon left her feeling, clear her mind and blot out Joe's nerve-jangling presence. The success of the operation depended on her ability to mask her professionalism while she secretly drew upon it. Cici Baron, a slightly air-headed woman madly in love with her husband, would sail along on the surface. Underneath, Special Agent Leighton would calculate how to ensnare her target.

She drew out a gold compact from the bottom of her designer bag. Glittering diamonds formed the letter C on the lid. She opened it, checked her already perfect lipstick and smiled at her reflection—a hopeful woman ready to adopt a baby.

She beamed at Joe, her beloved Alexander. "Daddy, they just have to let us have a baby. Cici really wants a baby."

He turned toward her like she was his cherished wife. "Whatever my Cici wants, Cici will have." His face transformed with a wide smile that warmed his eye a smoky blue.

She gave him an easy smile, reassured by his apparent ability to slip into his role as her partner. "Thank you, Daddy."

Donaldson played his role, too. "Mr. and Mrs. Baron, we have arrived."

He hurried around the limo, opened the door and extended his hand to help Mrs. Baron out of the car.

Joe hopped out behind her, put his arm around her and drew her close to his side.

"C'mon, darlin'. Let's go get Cici a baby."

Secure with his hand on her waist, she let him steer her through the tangle of pedestrians on Park Avenue into the same compartment of a revolving door. He never let go of her as they spun through and stepped into line at the lobby security screening area.

They ambled linked together toward the elevator banks. The heels of her Jimmy Choos clicked on the marble floor. She noted the placement of each security camera. There were two in the elevator car. She nestled her head on his shoulder as they ascended to the top floor.

The bandage he wore brought out her protective instincts. She reached her hand up lovingly toward the gauze over his eye. "Does it hurt much, sugar?"

His hand deflected hers with a reflexive thrust

before she could touch it. But he converted the rebuff into a caress when he turned her hand and kissed her palm tenderly. He had noticed the cameras, too.

"Only hurts that I can't look at you with both eyes, Cici," he whispered. His breath warmed her sensitive skin.

Their eyes locked. A blush crept a scorching path up her neck to her cheeks. His touch left her lightheaded.

Glad his strong arm still supported her as the elevator doors swished open, she half-levitated into the plush office of Bradley Sterling. Exactly how she had pictured it: mahogany, priceless oriental rugs, eclectic antique furniture and major dollars elegance, the place screamed, "Look but don't touch." All meant to impress. She wasn't impressed with the room's décor, but she did appreciate the state of the art surveillance equipment discreetly and expertly camouflaged.

An older woman with a pinch face led them into Sterling's inner office. The man rose from behind a massive mahogany desk, his arm extended. Bobbie's head cleared and nothing mattered but the target.

He appeared tall until he moved closer to Joe. Six-one, Bobbie figured. Distinguished with each white-gray hair in perfect place and a smooth-shaven tan face, the impeccable Armani suit he wore draped his slender frame. A status Rolex circled the bronzed skin of his wrist. A glint reflected off the manicured nails of his outstretched hand.

He stood before them with a subtle click of the heels of his gleaming dress loafers and grasped Joe's hand, then hers, with cool nonchalance.

"Mr. and Mrs. Baron. This is a pleasure. Come sit down."

He led them to a grouping of leather chairs and couches in a corner of the massive room. An aura of citrus aftershave floated in his wake.

He arranged himself in an armchair and crossed

his legs...the unflappable stereotype of a got-rocks attorney.

Bobbie and Joe sat next to each other, thigh to thigh, on the cashmere-like sofa cushions across from Sterling. She plastered on a delighted smile and widened her eyes in Cici's brand of innocence.

"Can Martha get you something to drink?"

She fluttered her lashes. "Oh, Mr. Sterling. Thank you, no. I'm too nervous to drink anything. I don't think I could swallow. My land, I'm a wreck," she burbled in her south of the Mason-Dixon Line cadence.

"There's nothing to be nervous about, darlin'." Joe cupped her knee with his hand. "Mr. Sterling will help us."

"But Daddy, what if he doesn't like me?" She implored like a child.

"What's not to like, darlin?" Impassive, he faced Sterling.

"There is nothing in the world Cici wants more than a baby. I'm told you're the man to make that happen. Is that information correct?"

Sterling dismissed Martha with a hand wave. His attitude dripped calculated intimidation while the woman left his office. He waited until the door clicked shut behind her before he spoke.

"I have helped make arrangements for the right people." His lips widened in a smile that never reached his eyes.

"Is that a yes or no, Daddy?" Bobbie wrung her hands.

"I believe it's a yes, Cici. Isn't that right, Bradley?" Joe leaned forward. "I *can* call you Bradley?"

"You can call me Brad, or whatever you like," he said, unfazed. He hooked silver-framed glasses over his ears and picked up a file from the coffee table that separated their seats.

He nested the file on his knee and bent over it.

"We're among friends, Alex and Cynthia." He scrutinized them. "Let's take care of some paperwork first."

"Paperwork? Didn't my assistant send you everything you asked for?"

"Yes. I received all the information I needed. I wish to review a few things with you. You must understand that I have to take every precaution with my screening process. I need to make sure that any child I place will have the perfect home. I guarantee the selfless mothers I represent that their sacrifice is the right choice for their children. I'm dedicated to giving these children the kind of lives their natural mothers never could."

"The very reason we're here." Joe took off the cowboy hat and tossed it on the coffee table. He smiled at Sterling. "I assure you that our child will never want for a thing."

"You were recommended to me by a former client. How do you know the McKenzies?"

"Never met 'em." Joe glanced at Sterling, unperturbed.

"Stella McKenzie is my dear friend, even though we never get to see each other," Bobbie threw out.

A Sterling adoption that never took place had led the FBI to the McKenzie's and other Sterling clients.

"We were at Texas A&M together for a year. Until Ian proposed and she moved back to Virginia to get married. It wasn't two weeks later that I met my Alex at the rodeo. I guess Stella and I earned our Mrs. degrees, didn't we Daddy?" Bobbie beamed at Joe.

The terrified McKenzie's had agreed to back up Bobbie's story even though they might lose their child in the process. There had been no match in the databases with their baby and any reported missing child. The same held true for other Sterling adoptions. But the process for another couple that never adopted a Sterling baby had pointed the FBI toward Chicago—the basis for her assignment to the Sullivan funeral. The date Sterling refunded the couple's money and refused to continue working with them matched the date of Jimmy's cell phone call.

A week later Jimmy was murdered.

Cici warmed to her story. "Stella and I always send each other Christmas letters every single year. Stella sent me a birth announcement for little Tyler and I went shopping right away. Picked out the cutest little pair of sailor pants for him and these teensy little shoes. Just darling. Then Stella called to thank me and I confided in her how much I wanted to have a baby and she told me she didn't really have Tyler at all, but she adopted him. And then she told me how you helped her—"

"Yes. Lovely," Sterling interjected. "Let's move on, shall we?"

He glanced at a paper in the file, took off his glasses and dangled them in his hand. "You scheduled the home visit at a New York address. How do you plan to live here and run a Texas-based company?"

"Cici wants a baby now. Seemed smart for us to come to you." Joe shrugged. "And we're taking the company public. Works for me to be close to the financial folks for a while."

Joe picked up his hat and fingered the brim. "But if you'd rather a visit at Baron House, it's all the same to me."

Bobbie willed herself to breathe, just breathe. And smile Cici's adoring, vacant smile while the penetrating line between the two men held like a tightrope.

Sterling put on his glasses again. "That won't be necessary. New York will be convenient."

He flipped a couple pages in the file. "What happened to your eye? There's no documentation of an injury in your file."

"Should be." Joe's leg tensed, but his face remained perfectly calm. "Well, it's like this..." he grinned. "I could tell you a yarn about a macho bar fight or the bronco that threw me on my face, but truth is I had LASIK surgery. Botched from the get-go. Had to call in a surgeon to fix things before I lost sight in this eye permanently."

He brushed his fingers on the bandage's edge. "My doctor, Michael Lynch out of Chicago General, promises me that I will be able to remove this thing in a few weeks. Better be able to see when I do. This other eye is fine."

"Your doctor was in Chicago?"

"No, my doctor was in Austin. Did the job half-assed. Trust me he'll not be operating on anybody I know anytime soon. I needed the best surgeon. I found him in Chicago. Flew him down a week ago."

Her stomach clenched. Why did he mention Chicago? How could he use his brother-in-law's name? What if Sterling made a connection? She had to stop this exchange.

She snuggled closer to Joe on the loveseat and touched the bandage.

"I'm gonna miss my pirate." She giggled.

"I'll buy a patch and play pirate any time you want." He touched his lips to hers. The sensation sent shock waves through her overburdened nervous system.

Sterling cleared his throat. "Have the surgical report sent to me. Why adoption?"

She squeezed her eyes with her hand and made them water. "We can't have children." She pitched her voice in woeful lament. "We tried and tried, but we can't. Well I can have children but..." She trailed off, dropped her eyes and picked at her nail polish.

"It's okay, Cici. He knows. It's all in that folder there, isn't it, Brad?"

"Yes. Nothing to be ashamed of, Alex," the lawyer said.

"It's the damnedest thing," Joe said. "No sickness when I was a boy or anything. But still... Lab results don't lie."

Bobbie hid her quivering mouth behind a crumpled tissue, then dabbed at her dry eyes.

"What I meant by the question is have you investigated other means? In vitro fertilization, for instance? Is adoption a last resort decision?" Sterling asked.

"Look, Brad, are you going to help us or not?" Joe patted his jacket lapel. "I'm prepared to compensate you generously."

Sterling bristled.

"Now, Daddy, don't go getting all fussy to Mr. Sterling." She cast a disarming glance at Joe, then turned her attention to the lawyer. "We have all the love in the world to give a baby. Will you help us, sir? Please?"

Sterling held up his palm. "Of course. Everything seems in order. Tell me about the kind of child you want."

Bobbie sighed, enraptured. "Oh, I see her so clearly in my dreams. She has dark wispy hair and her daddy's big blue eyes. I already have matching Christmas sweaters on order. Don't shake your head, Daddy. You promised we could wear matching sweaters for our first family Christmas card picture."

"So you're looking for a female baby," Sterling said.

"Well, yes. Well, no. I'd like a son, too. No one takes care of his momma like a son. I picture him tall and of course he'll love growing up on the ranch with us and he'll want to take over the family business and he'll always treat me special just like his daddy does." She smiled, blatantly adoring.

"Brad, bottom line. Girl, boy, doesn't matter. We'll be happy with either." Joe checked his watch. "Are you the man to make this happen? I've gone ahead and made an appointment with another highly recommended lawyer. If you can't help us we need to leave now to make that appointment."

"No need to go elsewhere. I will be happy to make your dream of having a family come true."

Bobbie burst into tears. Joe laughed and pulled her against his chest.

"You're going to make a wonderful mother." He kissed her.

Lost in the moment, Sterling's office vanished in a blur of her longing—a genuine rather than staged response to Joe.

Bradley cleared his throat discreetly and they drew apart.

"I'm so sorry we forgot our manners, Mr. Sterling," Bobbie said.

"Nothing to be sorry about, Mrs. Baron. You just found out you're going to be a mother. Enjoy the moment."

"When can you make this happen?" Joe pulled a fat envelope from the pocket of his cashmere jacket and held it in his lap.

"I can't guarantee a date just yet. These things take time, and well they should. We want to be sure a mother has no doubts about choosing to let adoptive parents raise her child. It's for the best for everyone."

Joe handed the envelope to Sterling.

"There's a hundred thousand in there. That's your going rate according to Stella McKenzie. Call us the minute you have more information. Let's go, Cici. Time to celebrate."

"One moment." Sterling handed the envelope back to Joe. "I'll require a check for $10,000 as my retainer. I like to document any payments I accept. After the home visit, we'll move to the next step. Expect my representative at any time in the near future. If all goes well with that, you pay the remainder of the fee in cash to remunerate the birth mother."

Joe fumbled in his pockets. "Forgot my check book. Will you accept the retainer in cash?"

Sterling shook his head.

Cici grabbed for her purse and opened it. "Daddy, you'd forget your head. I'll write the check, Mister Sterling, if you're okay with a starter check. I just opened the account yesterday and I haven't received the printed checks yet."

Bobbie leaned the check booklet on her purse and scribbled.

Sterling accepted the check and stood. "I'll write you a receipt."

"That isn't necessary," she said.

"I insist."

She gestured at Joe to walk with her to Sterling's desk. "I will never be able to thank you, Mr. Sterling." Tears streamed down her cheeks. She held out her hand to the lawyer.

"It is my pleasure, Mrs. Baron. I'll be in touch soon."

Joe clasped Sterling's hand in a firm grip. "Thank you for your help. I look forward to closing this deal."

****

"What the hell is wrong with you? What were you thinking? Why did you have to pick Mike as your doctor? Why did you have to mention Chicago? Don't you realize that you just threw up a red flag? Sterling isn't an idiot. I won't be responsible for my actions if you've ruined this case." She delivered her diatribe in little more than a whisper as the happy couple strolled entwined to the waiting limo.

"Calm down, princess."

The smug expression on Joe's face fueled her anger. "Don't princess me." She flung open the back door of the car and almost knocked Donaldson down. "Get in."

Neither man questioned her. They obeyed.

"Look, Bobbie," Joe said. "I spoke with Mike and told him I would be using his name on a case. He's all set to verify that he's Alex Baron's new personal physician. Contrary to what you think, I'm a good cop. I know what I'm doing. I held my own in there. Sterling killed my brother. I know it in my gut. I want him more than you do."

She cut off further argument but still fumed, preferring anger to the softer emotions that warred inside her. The way Joe treated her when she snuggled close in Sterling's office had melted her heart. *Just an act.* Nothing but regret involved with Joe Sullivan again.

"Slick that he wouldn't take the marked bills," Joe said.

"Yeah. He's slick. Lily white on paper, too."

"Good thinking to open that account."

"I know what I'm doing."

"Just happen to have that kind of money lying around, princess?"

"Not your concern..."

"Mr. & Mrs. Baron, we're being followed. Where do you want me to go?" John's eyes met hers in the review mirror.

"Home," she retorted.

"Don't go home, Donaldson." Joe ordered, the command a military bark, all business. No sign of Alex Baron in the car with her. "We told Sterling we're going out to celebrate and that's what we have to do. Take us to the Hudson Hotel. There's a bottle of Perrier Jouet with Baron's name on it."

Bobbie slouched in her seat, passive and brooding. The Barons didn't exist. She and Joe were not a couple. The sooner she accepted that the better. Those delectable kisses and the warmth of his arm around her were part of his act. He could want her and cherish her only if she were someone else.

Chapter 8

"May I help you, miss?" The slender woman blew past Sergeant Nagle standing at the front desk and twisted the knob on the locked door that led into the squad room.

"Miss," Nagle boomed. "You can't go in there until I say you can. Are you looking for someone?"

"Sorry." She reversed and stood facing him over the high counter, a real looker. Thin. Kind of exotic. "Yes, I am looking for someone. I'm not sure if he's here."

"What's the name?"

"I don't know."

"Are you picking up a detainee or do you need to speak with an officer?"

"He is a policeman."

"Okay. We're making progress. What's it in regard to?"

"It's confidential. Please, can I just walk around in there?" She craned her neck and peered over his shoulder. "I'll know him when I see him."

Frustrated with the dead end conversation and the ringing phones he had ignored for the duration, Nagle bristled. "Look, miss. This is a police station. Help me out here. What does he look like?"

She closed her eyes. "Tall. Short sandy hair, cut a little too short. If you want my opinion he should let it grow a bit, it would soften his face."

He cleared his throat, impatient.

"Blue sparkling eyes with just a hint of mischief." She opened her eyes and smiled.

Nagel chuckled and turned around. "Sullivan!" he bellowed.

"Not now. I'm in the middle of something here."

"Someone to see you."

"Just send him back."

She sailed through the door Nagle held open and honed in on Sullivan. "That's him. Thank you for your help," she dismissed Nagle.

She hustled back to Sullivan who stood up at his cluttered desk in the corner of the squad room.

****

"How can I help you?" Brian took the outstretched hand, shook it. A strange warmth traveled up to his shoulder that left him slightly off center.

"I think *I* can help *you*," she responded.

He looked into her dark chocolate eyes, lost and found at the same time. He led her into Joe's dark office, flipped on the light, pointed to the chair in front of the desk and took a seat in his brother's duct-taped leather chair.

She sat and stared at him making him increasingly uncomfortable.

Who is this woman? She seemed familiar, but he didn't recall meeting her before. He surely would remember those soft eyes in that heart-shaped face. The honey-colored hair that trailed over her delicate shoulders and down her back tempted him to wrap it around his fingers.

"You came to see me. Why?"

"I have a message for you." She scanned the sterile room, a dreamy expression on her face.

"I'm sorry, miss... I didn't catch your name."

"Matilda. My name is Matilda Connors."

"Okay, Matilda. I don't want to be rude, but I really am in the middle of something. So if there is nothing else I can do for you..." He attempted to stand, anxious to get this weird woman out of there.

"Susan Anderson," she stated before he fully stood.

"What?"

"Susan Anderson."

"I thought you said your name is Matilda." He smiled then, sure he was the victim of yet another prank. "I get it. The guys put you up to this, didn't they?"

He didn't get the joke, and he'd have someone's head for putting him through this.

"Jimmy told me to tell you, Susan Anderson."

"Jimmy?"

"Jimmy Sullivan."

"You know Jimmy?"

"No, I never met him that is until this morning."

Brian kneaded his temple to soothe the monster headache building behind his eyes. "That's impossible. My brother Jimmy is dead." His heart would always clench having to say those words out loud.

"I didn't know that. My visions don't always involve the other side. I'm sorry for your loss."

"Okay, Matilda. I've had enough. I don't know who thinks this is funny, but I don't, and I would like you to leave."

She made no move to accommodate his request and continued her hypnotic stare directly into his eyes.

"He said you wouldn't believe me." She stood and closed the office door. "He said to tell you not to trust anyone with this information, only family. You can't trust anyone else."

"And he told you all of this, this morning?"

"Yes."

"Well, thank you, Matilda for coming and sharing that. I will make sure I only tell family."

He needed to get rid of this crazy woman. Yet he wanted her to stay. Who was crazier?

"Let me explain."

Before he could say anything else she held up her hand to silence him.

"Most people have a problem believing I have a gift. I see things—people, events. Sometimes pictures in my head, sometimes words. Past, present, future—the tense isn't always clear. Sometimes it's like a movie. Usually I've never met the people who come to me and quite often I don't understand the messages they ask me to share. I just deliver the messages and hope they're helpful. That's all I can do."

"So my brother came to you and told you to share this information with me?"

"Yes. Do whatever you want with this. He said his name is Jimmy Sullivan. He showed me a photograph of you wearing a police uniform and said I was to tell you that Joe needs to contact Susan Anderson about the Safe Choice Program. She wants her baby back and Jimmy wants to help her. Then he said to tell you not to trust anyone but family with this information."

Matilda stood and turned away from him.

"That's it?"

"Yep. That's it." She pulled the door open, hesitated and faced him.

"One other thing. He said to stop trying to get any more information off his computer. Just be happy you have the cheesecake recipe."

She left him with his mouth gaping, paralyzed with shock. His brain commanded him to pursue her, but he couldn't. Then he overheard Steve talking to her.

"Hi Doc."

"Hi, Stephen. How is Snickers?"

"He's doing great, Doc, thanks."

"Wonderful to hear. Have a good day."

"You, too, Doc."

Steve stuck his head into Joe's office. "Hey Bri. Want anything? I'm doing a dinner run. You okay? You look like hell."

"Uh, yeah. I'm good. You know the woman who just left?"

"Sure. She's my vet. Craziest thing. My Lab kept getting sick. No one could figure out what was wrong with him. I brought him to Doc and she looked at the dog for a few minutes, real intense, and told me to stop giving him chocolate. I told her we didn't give him chocolate but she said, 'He's eating M&M's every day.'

Well, the wife keeps a bowl of M&M's on the coffee table. That dog was taking a few out at a time so we wouldn't miss them. Smart, huh? We took the bowl off the coffee table and the dog hasn't been sick a day since. Doc is amazing."

"Seems so. Oh, and Steve...remind me never to eat anything you put on your coffee table."

Chapter 9

Bobbie stared at the reflection of her bleary, bloodshot eyes. Her head pounded. Why had she matched Joe flute-for-flute of phony-celebration champagne? It was stupid to compete with him. What the hell happened last night?

She closed her eyes and splashed icy water on her face to banish the after-effects of her juvenile behavior. Fitful sleep and a rolling stomach all night left her weak-kneed and exhausted.

Joe, however, still snored a racket in the living room. She flip-flopped between wanting to go kick him awake and to curl up next to him—to lay her aching head on his shoulder.

Bobbie gagged her way through brushing her teeth, ran her fingers through her tangled hair and shuffled out of the bathroom over to her dresser.

She topped a one-piece, black spandex running suit with a Halloween orange, Texas Longhorns sweatshirt and stuffed her hair under a matching orange and white baseball cap intending to pound the hangover out of her system with a jog through the park.

The front door closed with a slight click behind her. Freedom!

Pushing through the revolving door out of the building lobby a cleansing lungful of air helped somewhat. It packed a frosty bite and made her eyes water, but she felt better already.

Time alone was a necessity for her every day. David had come to respect that after a while. In the beginning of their relationship he had wanted them to spend every free minute together. He had never understood her resistance to move in with him, and she still had a hard time explaining it, letting it suffice that it was a need for personal space.

Her childhood had forced isolation on her. But it had also given her the priceless gift of learning how to enjoy solitude, and as an adult she was never lonely.

Starting out in a lazy jog to let her muscles loosen and then increasing the pace as the knots and stiffness released, Bobbie had the city all to herself—just the way she liked it.

The own-the-world feeling blanked her over-active mind and gave her peace. In her temporary bliss, the case and her involvement with Joe dissolved amid the much-loved scenery. Past familiar shops bound for the loop in Central Park, the six-mile run unfurled.

Back to Manhattan after living in Chicago, Bobbie had sought out the familiar places, losing herself in Central Park many times as a day-off treat. Joe had distracted her all too frequently. Although she was determined to blot him out with thudding feet and aerobic breathing, he taunted her in the forefront of her mind.

Things could and should have been different between them. Why did he blame her for the loss of his eye? No one could have changed the actions of an unhinged killer. But Joe blamed her, even though they had never discussed that day again.

Nagging guilt persisted over owing him her life. He made her guilt-ridden. She had been grateful, had told him so, and probably would remain grateful to him forever.

Rapid footsteps approached from behind her. Bobbie edged to the far right of the path and hoped the runner would pass her. Some days the runners would exchange pleasantries but today wasn't her day to be sociable.

"Good morning, princess," came his booming voice.

It hurt her ears, made her cringe and earned Joe an angry glare.

"What the hell are you doing here?"

"Nice. Real nice. A little cranky today, are we? A wee too much bubbly for the southern belle?"

He jogged in place in front of her. The black sleeveless, under-armor shirt clung to rows of rippled muscle and a small patch of taut, tan skin showed above the waistband of his low-slung sweatpants. Delicious. Her gaze darted up above his waist, but it was too late.

He smiled that slow, sexy grin of his as if sensing her fantasy to lick that enticing piece of skin.

"I can handle a few glasses of champagne. Get lost. I want my trail to myself."

"Your trail? Well, your majesty, I wasn't told you owned Central Park. Does Donald Trump know?"

"You're a real riot. Now get lost."

"Would Daddy let his little Cici run alone?"

"Look, we don't have to be the Barons 24/7. We're not joined at the hip."

"Hmm...that sounds kinky."

"Stop it. I'm warning you."

"Warning me? Now, sugar, you should know better than to wave a red cape in front of me. I'll charge."

"I am not your princess. I am not your sugar. Now leave me alone."

"Sorry. No can do. I'm too professional. We do

have to be the Barons 24/7. What if you're being followed? Do you want to screw up the case because you're hung over and too ornery to play nice with Daddy?"

****

Of course he irritated her. He meant to. For some crazy reason he liked to see her neck muscles throb. That jutting chin and those pulsing muscles turned him on. A few more minutes and the temptation to tug off her sweatshirt would undo him.

"Look, let's just run," he said. "I need a break from Alex Baron, too."

"Fine, but don't talk to me." She set off down the path.

He caught up to her in a few broad strides.

"I did handle the champagne, didn't I?"

She didn't turn her head in his direction. A blush streaked her neck and reddened her cheeks. He knew exactly what she meant by the question and stifled the impulse to play to her unspoken embarrassment. For the moment.

"Yeah, sure. You drank me under the table."

He jogged along and let her stew.

She didn't know how far things had gone last night and must have been mighty confused when she checked what she wore under her bedcovers that morning. He had all but carried her to the bedroom after she swayed and teetered her way into the condo. She had stood in front of the bed with a brazen smile and very seductively unbuttoned her clothes, strip-tease style.

Lust scrambled his champagne-sodden brain as he watched, but somehow refrained from touching her except to catch her when she listed too far to one side.

She had slept in a scanty bikini and a couple of patches of lace for a bra. He had tucked her under the comforter before she could take anything else off.

With a sigh she had fallen dead asleep. Standing over her bed, he watched her innocent face for a while. Where he found the willpower to have left it at that, he still didn't know.

He would never have forgiven himself had he taken advantage of her total abandon to him. But he had wanted to shake her awake to get her conscious assent so he could caress that silken skin and grab fistfuls of her rosy hair. Instead he had softly closed the bedroom door and lain in his bachelor bed on the floor.

The mystery of what a couple scraps of material covered hung in his mind all night. It had been much the same story since he met her. He had never taken her to his bed. That knowledge had eased his conscience when he had turned away from her after his injury. He had all but told her he didn't want her then.

And had spent years wanting her.

When he had her in his bed they would be sober and in full control of the decision. *Where did that come from?* He had no intention of being in bed with Bobbie. Not drunk. Not sober. Never.

The sharp tone of her voice cut through. "Look, Sullivan. I want to know if anything ...uh...happened."

"No. You undressed yourself."

She nodded and inched ahead of him. The muscles in her butt tightened with each stride. Easy to say never, but damned hard to keep living it.

He trailed behind her. He didn't need a run. He needed a cold shower.

He caught up to her. "What's the plan for the day?"

"I told you not to talk."

"Come on. How about a truce? It'll break the monotony. Bet I can make you talk."

Her lips froze in a stubborn line.

"Fine. I hate small talk anyway. I'll just look at

your legs."

She clenched her jaw.

"Not exactly my type though. You're a little too muscular for me. I like my women soft and feminine."

"I'm as feminine as any wimpy, weak little girl that you might be dating." She stopped short, chest heaving.

"Probably could deck her with one punch, too." He smiled. "Gotcha."

She gave him a begrudging smile and turned forward on the trail to continue the jog. "You are the most infuriating man I have ever met. You're driving me crazy. Your poor mother and sister. How can they stand such a male chauvinist?"

"They think I'm the best. I'm my mom's favorite."

"I bet Brian, Danny and Patrick would tell me the same thing."

"I guess so. Mom always made us each feel special."

"You are so lucky."

"I know. I thank God every day for my family. Sometimes I want to kill my brothers but I love them."

He sucked in a breath against the stab of pain from his own choice of words. Someone had killed his brother. He grimaced and broke the rhythm of the jog.

All she did was touch his arm. The effect was like a soft salve on a burn. He appreciated it.

"Tell me what it was like growing up with all those brothers." Her voice was gentle.

"It was the best. We fought a lot but we had each other's back. If you messed with one Sullivan you messed with the whole family. I have to find out who killed Jimmy."

"I know."

They jogged.

"Look, I'm sorry if I've been tough on you. I don't believe Jimmy was dirty. I never did. You never gave me a chance to explain. I want to find his killer as much as you do."

"I get that now. We both want to nail Sterling."

"Might not be Sterling."

"It's him."

"We have to be sure. And we have to do this right."

"It'll be easier if we could do it without fighting each other."

"I agree," she almost sang. "As soon as you admit that I'm in charge we'll be very simpatico." She smiled over her shoulder at him and took off.

He laughed. She was worming her way under his skin again. Maybe he enjoyed that a little too much.

He pumped his legs and overtook her.

"First one to the fountain pays for breakfast."

He didn't wait for her answer to his challenge. He sprinted off but held back just enough to let her catch up and make a race out of it. He wouldn't let her win. He'd let her come close.

"You're lucky I stuck some cash in my pocket," she huffed as she reached the fountain split seconds behind him. "I'm too sweaty to eat out. Let's grab a cab and hit Zabar's for croissants. I'll make you an omelet to go with them back home."

"Deal. I never pass up a home cooked meal."

Home. I could get used to that, but I won't.

As soon as she helped him collar Sterling he would be back in Chicago fighting to return to the force. Fighting to get his life back. He was in this game with Bobbie for many reasons. Setting up housekeeping wasn't on the list.

He needed to remember that, but as he sat so close to her in the back of the cab, it was easy to forget.

"Wait a minute." She turned toward him, her

face the picture of distress. "How did you know I undressed myself last night?"

"You performed a pretty good strip tease. The only thing missing was music."

He laughed at the look of horror in her wide, almond eyes.

****

Brian Sullivan pushed papers around his desk after he left the third message for Joe. He had attempted to reach his brother since late last night and again since five this morning. Joe was an hour ahead in New York. Why wasn't he up yet?

Still the only one at the station house, Brian poured his second cup of coffee, not bad since he made it himself. The reason for his urgent calls to Joe rattled him.

Had it only been a day since he'd received the weird lead? He grabbed the phone and once again jabbed in Joe's number.

****

"Please detective, I want out. I can't do this anymore. These girls don't always want to give up their babies. Some of them want them back. But they can't find them if they change their minds. I won't say anything to anyone. You can trust me. Just don't ask me to pick up any more babies and bring them here. Let me put them in the system."

"I understand Sophie. I really do. It breaks my heart to see these innocent children abandoned, but I know they are going to a family that can give them a better life. It's much better than foster care."

I thought this one would work out. She needed the money.

"You have been such a big help so far, Sophie. Do you need more money? Is that what this is about?"

"No. It isn't right. We have a system at the department. And this...this feels like kidnapping or something. I just can't do it anymore. I can't sleep. I can't eat."

"Okay, I don't want you making yourself sick. Can I ask you for just one favor though?"

"What?"

"I haven't been able to deliver the baby you gave me on Thursday. I think she's sick. Can you come with me to look at her? I don't want to take her to a doctor unless you think I should."

So damn easy to get the ungrateful bitch into my car. Like a cow being led to slaughter.

Chapter 10

"Taste this." Bobbie slid the plate across the table in front of Joe.

The heady aroma of the steamy eggs whetted his appetite for breakfast, but Bobbie's sweet-scented nearness made him hungry to substitute the omelet with a reprise of that strip tease.

"Is it poisoned?" he challenged her, focusing on the food.

She angled over his plate, sawed off a forkful of the omelet and popped it in her mouth. Her breast brushed the side of his arm. He lowered his eye, steadied himself and then met her eyes.

She grinned and chewed with exaggerated rolls of her jaw. Impish, her cheeks a pretty pink from the earlier exercise and radiant cooking heat. He wanted to nibble on her sweet-smelling flesh but settled for sampling the eggs.

Oozy cheese and creamy butter coated his tongue. "This is good." He scooped up another ample mouthful. "I'll need another jog. I just ate half a bag of those cinnamon things."

"Rugelah." She smiled, victorious. "Glad you like the omelet."

She had just pulled out the chair across from

him when the phone rang. Her hips swayed nicely beneath the taught material on her way to the counter.

Her southern accent hit him as discordant at first, then exactly right. *She's good.* He wondered if he'd have had the presence of mind to jump into the role if he'd beaten her to the phone.

Her spine stiffened and she swiveled toward him. She grimaced and mouthed, "Shit."

"What?" he mouthed back.

"Well, of course, that would be fine," she drawled. "We can't wait to meet you."

She nodded as she listened to the caller.

"I'll clear you with the security desk. Just come straight on up to the penthouse. See y'all in an hour or so."

She scowled at him. "Go get showered. Use my bathroom."

He ignored the order for the time being. "Who was that?"

"One of Sterling's minions. We're about to be inspected. Go get showered, I said."

"Do I have time to snap to attention and salute you first?"

"Funny. Where's your gun?"

"In your Tampax box."

Her face turned sunny and she snorted a laugh. "Well get it out of there and wear it."

Grim again, she instructed, "I doubt she'll frisk us but she might rummage through things. I don't know what to expect. We have to do this just right. Hurry, I want a shower, too."

"Hey, calm down." He put his hands on the sides of her arms, surprised at the blast of heat from the casual contact. "It's okay if it looks like we're enjoying a lazy morning. We're rich. We can afford to be lazy."

He smiled at her, but she didn't smile back.

"Cici wouldn't be caught dead looking like this. I

have to put on a pound of makeup, so help me here."

"Okay. Give me five minutes."

"I'll stow your bedding and clear the dishes."

The bracing cool water did little to alleviate the effects of seeing her in a bra and panties, and then the soft brush of her against his arm.

Aware that he played with fire, he wanted to retaliate and gauge whether or not heat blasts were two-way with her. He sauntered back into the living room wearing the eye bandage, his shoulder-holstered gun and the smallest towel he could tuck around his hips.

Her deer-in-the headlights stare, the swallow in her throat and her quick intake of breath gratified him.

"Put some clothes on," she croaked. "Over..." she wagged her index finger up and down, "...that."

She cut a wide berth around him and disappeared down the hall.

She had regrouped quickly but it was there. He smiled and shrugged into his clothes.

He dug into his duffle for his cell phone and switched it on. The voicemail signal trilled. He dialed up and listened to Brian's voice.

"...if you want in, you have to get here by seven."

He checked his watch. He could be back in Chicago in time if he left now. He went down the hall toward the master bathroom, then reversed direction. He wasn't ready to let her in on this. Not yet.

Back in the kitchen he rustled through a couple of drawers and found a pad and pencil. He scribbled a note, grabbed his jacket and left.

****

"Done with time to spare." The living room was empty. No sign of Joe in the kitchen, either. Bobbie ducked into the study and even barged into the hall bathroom without knocking on the closed door. He wasn't there.

"What the hell?" Standing in the hall, hands on her hips, she squinted in the direction of the kitchen and spied the pad on the counter. She strode over, picked it up and read Joe's scrawl.

Family emergency. You were in the shower. Figured you wouldn't want me to see you naked. Again. Don't wait up.

She ripped the top sheet off the pad and tore the small page into bits over the trash bin.

I will kill you, D-a-d-d-y. What the hell am I going to do now?

She grabbed the portable phone, scanned the recent call log and dialed the first number.

"Miz Williamson? This is Cici Baron. Silly me, I went and confirmed our meeting here and forgot that my husband had to leave to catch a flight to see his eye surgeon. Why it just flew right out of my head until he gave me a kiss with his overnight bag in his hand. I was so excited to meet you. Would it be convenient to reschedule our appointment? He'll be back tomorrow." Bobbie held her breath.

"I'm down in your lobby. I'll come up and we'll visit. Perhaps we can get him on the phone."

Bobbie hung up and jammed her hands into Cici's apron pockets.

****

Joe shivered as the cold wind whipped snowflakes into his face. In February, Chicago's "Windy City" nickname had nothing to do with politics.

Brian's message and Joe's subsequent conversation with him en route to La Guardia airport had set off a flurry of activity that culminated with Joe standing outside at O'Hare airport. The details were still murky, but he had gone on his faith in Brian's judgment that he had a credible lead in Susan Anderson. A quick call to Uncle Frankie after he hung up with Brian and here he was.

Brian's mud-colored Jeep pulled to the curb with a screech. Joe slid in, grateful for the heated passenger seat.

"Thanks for picking me up," Joe said.

"No problem. What happened to your eye?"

"What are you kidding me? Is that supposed to be funny?"

Brian furrowed his brow. "Funny? You have a bandage over your eye."

"Oh right." Joe touched the gauze. "Sorry. I forgot about this. I use it instead of the patch. Has to do with LASIK surgery. Part of the UC operation with Bobbie."

Brian zoomed away from the curb unperturbed by the horns and brake squeals from the cars he cut off. Joe instinctively put his hand out and held on to the dashboard.

"I hope Susan shows," Brian said.

"You think she might stand us up?"

"She was skittish on the phone. She doesn't trust me and she feels like Jimmy lied to her. Left her hanging.

"Do you have any idea how many Andersons there are in the greater Chicago area?" Brian let out an exasperated breath.

Driving free of the O'Hare arrivals labyrinth, Joe eased back in his seat.

"I narrowed it down to people living in a radius of Main and Washington around Jim's precinct. When she answered and said she was Susan, I fumbled some. I couldn't believe I was looking for a kid. Anyway that's what she sounds like on the phone."

"What made her agree?"

"Bottom line, she wants her baby. That outweighs her distrust."

The snow-dotted landscape blurred past the salt-smeared window of the jeep. Joe's body warmed more from the adrenaline flow from being on to a hot lead, than from the lukewarm air that puffed in weak bursts out of the Jeep's vents.

"How's everything else with you, Bri? What are you working on now?"

"Still that missing teenager case. We have nothing. Everything has been a dead end."

"Something will break, it usually does."

"Yeah, but you know the longer it drags on..."

Brian pulled into a space on the outer fringes of a sprawling shopping center. Heads down against the wind, they trod into the middle of the outdoor mall. Benches surrounded empty water fountains and snow covered flowerbeds.

Two figures huddled together on one of the benches.

"That's them," Brian said. "She said she'd bring the baby's father with her."

They approached the couple. Susan was virtually a child. The kid next to her, more boy than man, glared at Joe with macho defiance and tightened the protective arm he had around her shoulder.

"Hi. Susan?" Joe asked in a low, and he hoped, non-threatening, voice.

She nodded.

"I'm Joe Sullivan and this is my brother Brian. We're Jimmy's brothers. Thanks for agreeing to meet us. I want to help you. It's freezing here. Would you like to go inside somewhere to warm up?"

She shook her head. "No, this is fine." She shivered.

Brian surveyed the mall and walked off toward a coffee shop. Joe sat down on a bench facing Susan and the boy.

"You have a lot of brothers." She eyed Brian. "I liked Officer Sullivan. He insisted I call him Jimmy—real friendly. He said he would help, but then I never heard from him again."

"If I had known Jimmy was working with you

before he died, I would have contacted you."

Her eyes widened and she grabbed at her companion's arm, bunching some of his jacket's material in her fist. "What do you mean he died? How?"

"In the line of duty," Joe ad libbed. He kept his expression impassive. "Please tell me everything you told Jimmy. I want to help you, too."

She let go of her boyfriend's jacket and rested mitten-covered hands in her lap. Her posture was stiff, and her expression wary, but she smiled at him with pure innocence. Joe had a moment of piercing guilt because he didn't know if he might be exposing her to danger. He'd tell Brian to kept an eye on her and the boyfriend after he went back to New York.

"I had my baby and my mother wouldn't let me keep it. My dad left a couple of years ago and things are pretty tight at home," Susan said.

"When was this? Do you remember the date?"

"Of course I do. Bonnie—I named her Bonnie before my mother made me give her away—was born November 12th. I remember it because I was studying for my stupid Spanish test and all of a sudden my water broke and my mother rushed me to the hospital. Two hours later Bonnie came out."

"You had Bonnie in the hospital?"

"Yeah, sure. Where else?"

"You gave your baby up in the hospital?"

"No. We took her home the next day. My mom said she'd help me raise Bonnie, but after a couple days home with her crying all night, she told me that I had to turn her in to the Safe Choice Program. She made me."

Susan cried and the boy tightened his grip around her, looking helpless at the sight. Tears trailed down her red, chapped cheeks and fell on the striped scarf wrapped around her neck.

Brian came back with a tray of steaming cups, passed them out and sat down on the bench next to

Joe. Joe wrapped his hands around the cup, grateful for the warmth.

Susan accepted a cup and sipped at it, her hands shaking. She composed herself gradually.

"I brought the baby to the police station in Windsor Village," she continued. "The policewoman was so nice to me. She told me that I had forty-eight hours to change my mind and get my baby back."

"Do you remember her name?"

'No, I never asked her name and she didn't ask for mine, either."

"Okay. What happened then?"

"When I got home I called Rob at college and told him what my mother made me do. And he said he'd come home and we'd get our baby and get married. He came home the next day. We went back to the police station. They said no police woman worked at that station and there was no record that I dropped off Bonnie."

"Could you describe the police woman, do you think?"

"I don't know. Maybe."

"What did you do after that?"

"I begged my mother to help us, but she said it was meant to be and to get on with my life. Rob's parents just wanted him to get back to school. No one would help us. Then a couple of weeks later, Jimmy called me and asked me to tell him my story and he said he would help me find Bonnie."

"Did he say how he found out about you and your baby?"

"No. He just said he would help me."

"I want to help you, Susan. I can't promise you that I will find her, but I will do everything I can to track down Bonnie for you. If you need to get in touch with me, call Brian. He can reach me day or night."

"Thank you." A wistful smile lit her face.

The hope in her eyes touched Joe deeply. He

would not stop until he found out who took Bonnie and who killed Jimmy. It had to be the same person. Sterling? Pretty long reach from New York.

He sat on the bench with Brian as Rob led Susan towards the parking lot.

"Babies having babies. Makes you wonder if little Bonnie is better off where she is," Brian said.

"I don't know. I promised her I would help her and I will."

They returned to the jeep.

"What do you know about the Safe Choice Program?" Joe asked.

"No more than you do, probably. No questions asked, do a bunch of paperwork and then turn the babies over to Children and Family Services."

"Anyone you trust over at Windsor Village?"

Brian's mouth moved as if to speak, but he clamped his lips together.

"What?"

"Jimmy told us not to trust anyone but family."

"Right. He's channeling through that loon Marilyn."

"Matilda. Maybe she's a loon, but how did she know Susan's name? How did she know about the cheesecake recipe? It was freaky, Joe. I wish you were there when she told me. I didn't believe a word, but at the same time I knew it was true. Jimmy doesn't want us to trust anyone. There has to be a reason."

"You think we're dealing with dirty cops?"

"Maybe. Or somebody posing as a cop. I think we better be careful."

Joe glanced at his watch. "I better go or I'll miss the last flight back to New York."

"Can't you stay for dinner?"

"Nah. Wish I could." Joe had another moment of piercing guilt over leaving Bobbie behind and out of the loop, with no explanation.

Brian switched on the ignition and gunned the

car in reverse out of the parking space. They left the mall and headed back toward the airport.

The two brothers were quiet during the bulk of the trip, comfortable around each other without the need to converse.

Joe mulled over the details of the interview to piece together the trail that led Jimmy to Susan. The sequence evaded him. He focused on his futile attempt at data retrieval from Jimmy's computer, sure that the data trail had been there before it was destroyed.

"How are things going with the little woman?" Brian interrupted Joe's circular thinking.

Joe laughed. "Wow, you better never call her the little woman to her face. I'm pretty sure she'd shoot you."

"That doesn't sound like the sweet girl I remember."

"Trust me. She's a pain in the ass. Tough, ornery and a real handful."

"Sounds like someone is falling hard." Brian gave him a cocky grin.

"What? Me? No way." Joe remembered a floral scent, an impish smile, and a fringe of lace that touched a delicate swell of breast. He cleared his senses and banished the vision with a deep, audible breath that Brian picked right up on.

"Sure," Brian said, heavy on the sarcasm.

Brian stretched another toothy grin at him. "I expected her to show up with you today—the happy couple."

"She would have if she knew anything about this meeting."

"You didn't tell her."

"No."

"Shit, Joe. Better find out where her gun is." Brian chuckled.

Joe knew the reckoning with her would come—probably the minute he opened the door. "She'll sleep with it strapped on."

They pulled to the curb at airline departures.

"Where do we go from here with Susan Anderson?" Joe asked.

"I'll take a look at the females on the force. See if I can find any connection with Jimmy...show Susan some photos. I'm still trying to find Jimmy's cell phone."

"Good. Keep an eye on her and that kid, Rob, too, okay?"

"Yeah."

"I'll try to stay in touch," Joe promised.

He leaned over and hugged Brian.

Security was no problem thanks to Uncle Frankie. Joe had time before the flight boarded. He strolled by a jewelry store and browsed the display. Alex would buy Cici a little souvenir.

He chose a dainty necklace with a diamond pendant of double overlapping hearts: one large and one tiny. He paid with a credit card issued to Alexander Baron and tucked the bag in his jacket. He'd figure out where the bill went and give the money to Frank Monahan out of his own pocket when this was all over.

At the gate, the flight delay announcement estimated TOA at LaGuardia around 1:30AM. He checked his cell phone. Not good. He had five missed calls, all from the phone number of the penthouse, and one message.

He connected to voicemail and waited. He expected to hear Bobbie's voice hurling expletives, so he was surprised to hear Cici's twang instead.

"Daddy, please call your sugar. The nice lady is here doing the home visit for Mr. Sterling. She wanted to at least meet you by phone."

Bobbie's muted voice drawled, "He's probably on the plane now." An indecipherable female voice sounded in the background.

"I hope everything goes well with your doctor's

appointment. I miss you. I love you," Cici said loud and clear. Bobbie hung up—he imagined by damned near splitting the phone in half on one of the kitchen counters.

She'd definitely sleep with her gun strapped on.

****

He should have been exhausted by the time he reached the penthouse. Still wired from the meeting with Susan, he was wide-awake. When he saw the ribbon of light beneath the double doors, he was glad he had an adrenaline high going. He'd have to be alert to deal with Bobbie.

Chapter 11

"Honey, I'm home." Joe eased through the door in a semi-crouch just below the trajectory of a crystal vase. It hit the door jam with a heavy thump and fell on the carpet. A book followed the vase and hit its mark.

"Hey, that hurt." Joe rubbed his shoulder as he dodged a sneaker.

"Good. It was supposed to hurt."

Bobbie stood on the far side of the coffee table. Strands of hair tumbled out of the rubber band at the back of her head and trailed over her shoulders, down her back. Her oversized T-shirt barely reached her thighs and slipped lower off her shoulder with each toss of assorted heavy stuff, aimed to crack his skull. Breathing hard, she paused, steaming. She picked up another shoe and let it rip. It went wide.

Joe waited, poised to dodge again. When no flying objects whizzed by, he stood upright and relaxed enough to take off his jacket. She faced him, gloriously defiant, an Amazon woman. Her shirt strained against her chest with each breath and her dark, hard nipples were visible through the tight material.

"Damn. That made me hot." His arousal pushed

against his snug, black denim jeans. Her eyes traveled from his chest downward and a grin lit up her face.

"You want hot? I'll give you hot." In one swift motion she picked up a mug off the table and whipped it towards him, a perfect strike.

Lucky for him he still held his jacket in his hand. He swept it up like a toreador in front of his face. The coat took the brunt of the hit, but hot liquid splattered on his hands.

"Ouch. Damn. Stop it." He dropped the wet coat on the floor. His hands burned and he wiped them on his thighs to stop the heat. It had the opposite effect on his arousal.

Her eyes whipped around, apparently searching for something else to throw at him and tugged at the pillow on the back of the sofa. When it didn't give, she hopped up on the seat cushion and yanked at it harder. *If she realized how seductive she looked, she'd stop doing that.* A glimpse of lace panties made him groan.

"Honey, add a sorority sister and a little water on the front of your T-shirt and you have everyman's wet dream. You're killing me here."

The fury mounted on her face and he laughed.

She stepped down from the couch and stormed off to the kitchen.

"I'm sorry. I'm not laughing at you." No response from the kitchen.

Gathering together the launched items, he stacked the books and magazines on the coffee table and tucked her shoes beneath. He kicked off his shoes and placed them in a neat pair next to hers before settling on the couch.

It's fun to goad her. "While you're in there could you grab me a beer?"

Realizing a little too late why she had marched to the kitchen, a plate swished past inches from his ear and crashed against the bookcase.

"Damn." The next plate hit him in the shoulder.

"What is wrong with you? Stop it."

"What is wrong with me? With me? You take off. Leave me here alone to face the home inspection. And you are stupid enough to ask me what is wrong with me?" Each sentence was punctuated with the crash of a dish around him.

Hands empty, she disappeared again, surely on her way to stock up on ammo.

Keeping low to the ground, he crab-walked to the kitchen door. She reached for a dish on the high shelf, putting her off guard to his forward rush and arm-lock maneuver.

While her arms were pinned, Joe talked fast. "I'm sorry, Bobbie. I had no choice."

She wiggled against him, trying to break free, but he tightened his hold. She retaliated with a head butt attempt.

"No way, princess." He flattened his hand on the crown of her head. "You broke my nose once. I'm not stupid enough to let you break it again." Easily lifting her squirming body, he carried her over to the sofa.

"I am so mad at you," she hissed between clenched teeth.

"Really? I hadn't noticed."

Matters only worsened with his cocky retorts. She kicked out, causing him to lurch sideways, off balance. He wouldn't let go of her, but couldn't compensate without his arms free.

The momentum sent him over the couch's arm onto seat cushions, taking her with him. His elbows jutted out at splayed angles, taking the brunt of his weight. He landed hard on them, on top of her. Her lithe body heaved beneath him. Her eyes glowed wild and her hair tumbled like fire around her face. She stared up at him.

Everything changed in that one moment. Desire swamped him. He dipped his head and tasted her lips, tea and sweet honey. Her body tensed, unyielding.

She struggled and pitched. But he planted his lips on hers again to tempt her to come with him in another kind of freefall. Then she softened like the gathering roll of a wave under him, and they both went under its crest when she returned the kiss.

Dizzy, intoxicated by the lush scent, taste and feel of her, he let his guard down. With a sudden arch of her back and kick of her legs she toppled him off her. His tailbone hit the floor. His head swung back and landed with a brain-scrambling thump between the coffee table and the sofa. She rolled down on top of him and straddled his hips, victorious.

Her tousled hair around her shoulders; her eyes flashed smoky and triumphant. She looked him dead in the eye with an unspoken dare to try to stop her from unsnapping his jeans and pulling them down.

Paralyzed, helpless, all he could do was lie there, watch her and let her take control of what came next.

Her eyes locked on his. She reached her hand down and touched the crotch of her panties. Slowly, she pulled the thin line of lace aside and mercilessly slid her body down over him in aching degrees. Her body opened to surround his erection and fuse them together.

A groan escaped his clenched lips and he shut his eyes, lost in her velvet softness. It took total concentration not to come immediately like some pimply-faced teenager. Just as he was able to muster some control, she moved, slowly at first, up and down, painfully slow, propelling him near the limits of restraint.

She rose up just short of freeing him from her body's grasp, then slid slowly back down, rocking him senseless. He reached under her T-shirt. His hands skimmed up to her soft bouncing breasts. Her nipples hardened like pebbles under his palms. She moved faster. Her groan of pleasure loosened his rein on self-discipline.

He didn't want to hold back. His hands slid down and grasped around her hips to lock their bodies closer. Her head threw back, her silky-smooth throat stretched to the limit as she tightened around him with each thrust.

She was close to release, but he knew her. She would ride him all night until he surrendered first. Their eyes locked and he read the stubbornness and defiance in hers. She was in control now. She wanted to win. He'd let her. He was incapable of prolonging the explosion building inside him.

Her muscles clenched him like a vise. He relinquished any remnant of free will he had left and released, just as she quivered and met him in exactly the same dazzling place. Suspended for a minute, for eternity, time froze. There was just this moment, just them. Her body held his captive as she dropped her head down on his chest. Her heart pounded against his ribs. He held her close, her body fitted to his as if they had melted together.

"Wow." She whispered, her warm breath rippling his chest hair.

"You can say that again."

"Wow." She stirred as if to pull away, but he tightened his arms. He didn't want this to end, not yet.

"I'm not going to apologize."

"Okay."

"You deserved all the things I threw at you."

"Honey, you can throw the whole apartment at me, as long as it ends with me under you, while you have your way with me."

She laughed. "Seems to me you gave as good as you got."

"Thanks. Then I'm not going to apologize, either."

Quiet. Her skin cooled as he rubbed his hand over her back where her shirt rode up. What was she thinking? Was she regretting her actions? He hoped not. He didn't regret one glorious moment. They should probably move.

"This shouldn't have happened."

Probably not, but he didn't want to hear it.

She continued, "We're undercover officers. What about the code of conduct?"

"Honey, you forgot about the code when you threw the first dish. Rule number one—avoid doing bodily harm to your partner." He smiled at her but she obviously didn't appreciate his wit.

She wiggled off him and shimmied to squeeze into the tight space. He didn't want to let her go but had no choice. He sat up, moved over to give her room and pushed the coffee table out of the way with his shoulder. She sat up on the couch, perched over him.

God, she's beautiful with her swollen, dark cherry lips, her pink-streaked cheeks, her fiery mass of curls and her T-shirt hung off her shoulder. She sat quiet and pensive.

"What are you thinking?" He asked, hoping it was anything other than regret.

"I'm still thinking about the code."

"And? I'm not going to report you if that's what you're worried about."

"Actually, I'm thinking, what the hell? If I broke it once, why not break it again?"

She laughed and offered a hand down toward him. He took it and hoisted himself up. She pulled him towards the bedroom. He didn't resist.

Right then, he would follow her anywhere.

****

Bobbie released his hand and stood next to the bed, feeling self-conscious and vulnerable, despite her boldness minutes before. Her eyes met his. The remembered "old Joe" sweetness in his ocean blue eye elated her.

Pulling her shirt slowly over her head and standing in front of him in her lace panties, his eye darkened and his jaw clenched.

He reached out and slid his rough hands over her shoulders and down the sides of her arms. He took her hands in his, circled them around his neck and pulled her close to his chest. She thrilled at the contrast of her pliant breasts against the hard planes of him.

His kiss touched off shimmering spasms at her core. His tongue slowly traced her lips and nipped her lower lip with his teeth.

"Oh Bobcat, what you do to me," he whispered.

He lowered his head and took possession of her breast with his mouth. His tongue teased her nipple. Her legs went weak with the surge of longing.

Lying where he gently placed her on the bed, heat spiked higher with each article of clothing he shed and tossed on the floor. Her body fevered and opened at the sight of him, naked and fully aroused. He lay down next to her, and she rolled on top of him to begin the dance that would get him inside her again.

"Uh-uh." He nudged her onto her back. "It's my turn to break a few codes. I'll drive *you* crazy now."

"Did I drive you crazy?"

"I'm pretty sure you know you did. Let me return the favor."

He smiled as he propped himself over her and lowered his head. Leisurely he used his tongue on the flesh taut over her ribs. Beard stubble sometimes tickled, sometimes scraped tender skin inciting quaking waves of lust within her. Eyes closed against anything to distract from the delicious sensations, he nibbled and kissed a sensuous trail past her waist. Her hips moved in slow rolling, pulsing need.

Teeth grasped the lace waistband of her panties

and tugged. The comforter in her fists, every muscle in her body tightened. Crazy wasn't the word for what he was doing to her. Control evaporated as he nestled his head between her legs.

"You are beautiful." His hands gently opened her up. He lowered his head and his tongue brought her over the edge. Her toes stretched towards the bottom of the bed and her back arched off the mattress. She grasped his head and held him, urging him to move faster, embarrassed by her brazen moves but desperate for him to feed her mounting need. Waves of bliss flowed and ended on a moan.

"Joe, Joe, oh my God, Joe," she gasped.

As the ripples of pleasure waned, he slid up her sweat-slicked body, entered her and filled her. He braced himself over her, his eye locked on hers, and slowly plunged deeper and deeper.

With no conscious effort, their rhythm synchronized. She wrapped her legs around him, locked her ankles over his back and clasped his broad shoulders. They climbed together. His body poised on the brink, an invitation for her to catch up with him. She accepted, and they reared up and free fell over the edge together.

Her eyes clamped shut, she floated out of the sweet ecstasy while their bodies still remained joined. Joe moved off her and settled next to her. Cold without the blanket of his body over her, she cuddled against the warmth of his chest and pulled the down quilt over them, content to savor the feel of his arms around her. His breathing slowed.

She relaxed in a blank, dreamy state. She had nearly fallen into a doze when her mind cleared. She couldn't let him drift off to sleep without an explanation for sticking her with a solo home inspection.

"Don't think for one minute that ..." She paused for a moment, unsure what to call what had just happened. Sex? Making love? Both? "That what we just did changes anything. I'm still furious."

"Sure you are. Me, too, for all those flying objects bombarding me." He tugged her tighter in his arms.

"Where the hell did you go? Why didn't you leave a message or something?"

She pushed up on one elbow.

"Chicago. Didn't you get the note?" He didn't open his eye.

Her gut twisted with alarm. His note had referenced a family emergency. "Is everybody okay?"

"Sure. They're fine." He stretched one arm over his head and yawned. He squinted up at her. "I promise I'll explain everything in the morning." He closed his eye. "Let's sleep for a while."

The gauze over his eye had slipped. One piece of tape held it to the skin high over his eyebrow. She reached over, tenderly removed the bandage with a gentle flick, and revealed his puckered scar in the middle of a convex pocket of skin. She wanted to touch it, kiss it, and show him it didn't matter.

His hand shot out from under the covers and grabbed her hand. His other hand slapped the gauze back and held it in place. He was on his feet and moving fast away from the bed.

"You don't need to wear that with me, Joe. We're partners," she said to his back.

He turned and faced her. "I don't do partners."

"You do now."

"I work alone."

She believed him. She would be a fool to think otherwise after his behavior today. Perhaps she was a fool in general. But she'd think about that later. "Screw you Sullivan."

"You just did." He stalked away and slammed the bedroom door behind him.

Chapter 12

Bobbie nudged Joe in the side with her big toe. He surfaced instantly from a dead sleep on the living room floor. One fluid roll away from her and he was on his feet, tensed, and poised to draw on her like a gunslinger with dead aim from his penetrating eye.

Admirable reflexes. She glared at him with equal force. His gaze softened, an almost imperceptible flash of yielding to her, and then froze solid. He wore his eye patch. A fleeting image of the scarred eye socket beneath it briefly shook her resolve to be as hard as he was. He stared at her and she recognized the implacable son of a bitch that he obviously was at heart. She could be implacable, too.

He was bare-chested and the loosely tied sweat pants he wore dipped too low on his narrow hips for her not to notice just where the material hung. The unsteadying inner plummet of attraction to him didn't matter. That was just chemistry. What mattered is that she had let her guard down with him and mistook hormones for heart-song. She wouldn't let that happen again.

"Put some clothes on. We have to talk." She took the first "shot."

"No." He swiveled toward the window, his back

to her.

"It isn't a request, Sullivan, it's an order," she fired again.

He spun back in her direction. A muscle in his jaw jumped. "Which part, *Agent* Leighton? I dress at your command or I talk?"

"Where were you yesterday?"

"Chicago. I already told you."

"Doing what?"

"Investigating a lead."

"In my case?" The volume of her voice upped per word.

"Our case as you so often tell me."

"Okay, *our* case. How come *you* handled *our* lead when *our* is the operative word?"

He scrubbed his hand up over his face from his nose to his brow. He stared back at her with a helpless expression, his fingers in his hair.

She would *not* break eye contact and she would *not* back down even the smallest fraction of an inch. She waited, silent.

"I'm sorry, Bobbie."

If the apology were remotely condescending or falsely conciliatory she would have flown at him in fury. But it wasn't. It was sincere and it was tender. The latter shook her. That he was capable of tenderness tempted her to compose heart-songs in her head again. But she couldn't orchestrate a harmonious duet with Joe.

She sat down at the dining room table, hands folded in front of her. "Apology accepted," she said. "Do I get the facts?"

"Yes." He sat down across from her. "Brian asked for help in questioning a girl Jimmy was working with, roughly a couple months before he was murdered. I believe now it got him killed."

"Who and how?"

"Susan Anderson is the girl's name. Jimmy gave Brian the lead through a psychic, I guess you'd call her."

She rolled her eyes. "Brian's into séances? What's that all about?"

"Look. It doesn't matter how we found the girl. She gave her baby to a female officer, regretted it the next day and hasn't seen her kid since. Jimmy somehow found out about it and contacted her. He promised to help her. Didn't live long enough to keep the promise. Explains the cell phone link to Sterling. I'm guessing Jimmy hacked phone records. Sterling snatches these kids before they're in the system. That much is clear."

"Tell me about the system."

"It's called Safe Choice. Women who otherwise would abandon their babies can turn them over to hospital or law enforcement personnel anonymously. The women aren't prosecuted and it keeps babies out of dumpsters. They're placed in foster care."

"All right. We're probably dealing with other supply points for Sterling...other programs like these." She folded her arms and leaned back in the chair, pensive. "What records are kept?"

"Brian is doing more legwork. I'll get copies of the paperwork that's used in Illinois. There are similar programs in other states, but I don't know what they're called."

"I'll call the Field Office and get Donaldson working on matching the Mackenzie kid with any of these kinds of programs nationally."

"Fine, but you'll come up empty. Susan was told there were no records when she went to get the baby back."

"We'll just have to hope we have more luck tracing where our kid came from."

"Our kid? How did the home visit go?"

The temporary thaw froze over and Bobbie's conflicting feelings with Joe resurfaced—hurt, regret, anger.

"Great, no thanks to you." She wanted to blast a

hole in him. She wanted to pull the cord on his sweat pants and wrestle him to the floor.

The professional in Bobbie won out. "My take is that the home visit was legit," she said. "The woman seemed sincere that she wants good homes and loving people for Sterling's adoption placements. I don't think she has a clue what Sterling's all about."

The doorbell rang with a symphonic flourish. She backed away from Joe toward the door, irritated at the interruption. It had to be one of her men; otherwise somebody from the security desk would have called.

She flung open the door ready to pounce on an underling and faced "Miz" Williamson instead.

"Dear me," Cici sputtered. She plucked at the sleeve of her sweatshirt, grateful that it was an ordinary solid gray with no telltale logos. "Come in, ma'am. I look a sight. Why in the world didn't security call up to let me know to expect you?"

"I just told that nice man down there I knew the way up and I wanted to surprise you. He recognized me from yesterday," she chirped. She stepped into the hallway.

So much for a swanky security system. Bobbie accompanied the woman down the hall while her mind raced thinking about Joe's bedding on the living room floor. She didn't breathe as she led Sterling's investigator toward him.

She exhaled, relieved, at the sight of him. He had spread his blanket out and he lay on his back, doing ab crunches. Miz Williamson was mighty impressed. There was no mistaking the female avarice in her expression.

Amused, Cici exchanged sly glances with her. "He's a yummy one, isn't he?" she said under her breath. "Daddy, Miz Williamson from the agency is here to meet ya."

The woman smiled back at Cici as Joe hustled to his feet. He stretched a hand toward Williamson.

"Glad to meet ya, ma'am. Sorry I missed you yesterday."

Williamson clasped Joe's hand and allowed him to turn hers, draw it toward him and peck the back of it with his lips.

"Please call me Virginia." She beamed at him. "Your wife and I had a nice visit yesterday, but I couldn't approve the adoption until I met you, too, Mr. Baron."

"Of course, Virginia." Joe stood in front of the two women, not the least bit self-conscious about the extent of rippled abdomen on display. "But please..." His face split in a sunshiny grin. "Call me Alex."

"Daddy, you should put on a shirt," Cici said pointedly.

"No need, no need." Virginia fluttered a hand in the air.

Joe padded toward the bedroom.

Bobbie turned toward the kitchen. "Why don't you come along with me and sit at the kitchen counter while Daddy changes?"

Virginia followed her into the gleaming room.

"I'll fix up some breakfast for us all," Cici chattered. "I have fresh coffee and I can fry up an omelet in no time."

"I'm not staying, Mrs. Baron," she replied. But she sat at the counter anyway. "Coffee does sound good, though."

Bobbie poured three mugs and glanced up when Joe reemerged from the back of the apartment. He wore jeans and a biceps-grabbing T-shirt. Every bit as yummy as five minutes ago.

Williamson wiggled like a puppy in her seat as Joe sat down next to her. She took a sip of her drink, her eyes on him wide with worship.

"I hope that my absence yesterday didn't jeopardize our place in line to adopt a baby," Joe said, oozing southern honey. "I could never forgive myself if I was responsible to keep my darlin' waiting a day longer than necessary."

"Not at all." The woman literally basked in Joe's presence. She leaned closer to him. "I went out on a limb and already certified your home visit for Mr. Sterling. I just didn't feel a hundred percent good about it until I met you, too, Mr. Baron. Alex." She beamed at them, pleased with her announcement and the man who flanked her at the counter.

"Did you hear that, Cici, love?" Joe stood and planted one huge hand flat on the counter. He hurdled over the granite and grabbed Bobbie under each arm. He pressed her up toward the ceiling like she was a dumbbell. Hanging over him with phony adoration sizzling between them, she wanted to let go of a little drool aimed smack at his eye.

He eased her downward and let her loose. He winked across the counter at Williamson and held an outstretched palm in Bobbie's direction. A jewelry box had materialized in its center. "Happy Valentine's Day, sweetheart. Open it."

"Oh, Daddy, you shouldn't have." Bobbie focused on the box, uncertain that if she met the woman's eyes she could convince her that anything other than venom flowed in her veins where Joe was concerned.

She flipped the box open and let Joe enact the sweeping display of fastening the necklace around her throat.

"You have my heart and now our baby's."

The diamond hearts against her collarbone twinkled in the downcast light. Bobbie covered the "treasure" with one hand. "It's beautiful. Thank you, Daddy."

"Nowhere near as beautiful as you are, honey." Alexander Baron gazed at Cici adoringly.

"Time for me to leave," Virginia announced with a sigh and a misty-eyed smile.

Bobbie conjured up tears, too, as she showed the woman to the door. It was easy to cry. Cici had what Bobbie longed for—her man's heart.

Leaning an arm against the closed door, Bobbie expelled a breath to regroup before turning towards Joe. He stood a few feet away, backlit by glare from the bank of windows behind him. His face in shadows, she couldn't see his expression and drew closer.

He was unmasked for the moment. No Alex, no Daddy and no cocksure detective, just Joe. She missed "just Joe," missed his openness and sweetness, and had dreamed about what it would be like in his arms but hadn't come close to the reality.

Bobbie loved just Joe.

A switch flipped, his features hardened, his posture shifted and the cocky detective was back. "Did that all meet with your approval?" Had she revealed too much contemplating him? Was that the reason for the steel barrier he threw up between them?

Her gaze was level as she brushed by him. "You did fine. I'm going to get dressed."

Distance, perspective...I'm out of here.

****

"Where are you going?" he called, before she could make it fully through the door.

"Out."

He cornered her as she reached out a hand to hit the elevator button. "Out where? Aren't you a little...red?"

Clad head to toe in crimson: mini-skirt, cashmere sweater, opaque tights and Manolo Blahnik heels, Cici retorted, "It's Valentines Day, remember?"

"Ah."

"See ya."

She punched the button. He held her wrist. "Where?"

Disengaging her arm when the elevator door opened, the attendant garnered a smile from her as she swished inside the car.

With a toodle-oo wave goodbye, she fired her parting salvo, "I'm going to visit David, Daddy. I'll send him your love."

The elevator doors closed with a satisfying swoosh before he could respond to the jab. *Was he smart enough to know she'd never jeopardize her cover?*

Bobbie called John as the elevator descended and asked him to bring the car around. Before leaving the lobby, she considered reprimanding the security guard for being lax with Virginia Williamson earlier, but convinced the woman was harmless, it wasn't worth it.

John pulled up, and although she wanted to just get into the back seat of the car like a normal person, she waited, Cici-style, for him to handle the door open-and-close ritual.

"Where to, ma'am?" he asked, back in the driver's seat.

"Just drive for a while."

He glimpsed askance over the seat. "In Manhattan? You could walk faster."

"Yeah, okay.... How about Fifth Avenue? Cici can wander around the shops and waste time."

A red flimsy teddy in Bergdorf's prompted the wistful notion of wrapping herself up in it for Joe's Valentines Day gift. The underwear was tossed back in the display case along with any intensions of repeating last night's lovemaking with Joe.

The day was a waste, nothing but the pretense of enjoyable window-shopping. Underneath the mindless veneer, Bobbie dissected all the events of the last twenty-four hours until she processed them and filed them away.

She went back to the Upper Eastside at sunset, resolved to a strictly professional relationship with Joe, and eager to nab Sterling so she'd be finished with Alexander "Daddy" Baron.

****

Enticing, appetizing aromas greeted her return to the penthouse. Andrea Bocelli's voice wafted aloft below the high ceilings and a distinctly less tuneful tenor wafted from the kitchen.

She turned the corner into the room and found Joe at the stove, back to her, stirring sauce and singing oh so *profundo*. "Joe?"

He turned, angling the dripping spoon over the pot and gave her an accusatory look. "Did you see David?"

She tossed her too red purse on the center island. "No, of course not."

"Didn't think so." He turned back to the stove. "There's a glass of wine for you on the counter."

She noticed a bowl of gardenias next to the goblet of wine. She sniffed them after she took a sip of cabernet. "Alex has been busy today."

He turned his head toward her. "They're from me."

"Yeah, thanks Daddy." She took another sip of wine.

He left the spoon in the pot and folded his arms over his chest. "I said they're from me. I'm sorry. I shouldn't have cut you out from following up the lead in Chicago and I shouldn't have—"

"Don't." She held up her hand, terrified that the next word out of his mouth would negate what happened between them last night. "I accept your apology. And thank you for the gardenias. They're my favorite flowers."

"Look, we need to talk."

"Why? Did Brian find out anything relevant?" She went to the stove and leaned over the fragrant pot for something to do other than face him.

"No. We need to talk about last night."

She turned and squared off with him. "Last night was great."

He arched his brows.

"Better than great. But I think we can agree

that we were carried away and we won't let it happen again. Bad timing, you know?"

He leaned against the counter, appearing to debate with himself before he asked, "David?"

"Yes," she lied. "Can we work together as partners? Nothing more?"

She saw evidence of the inner debate in him again. He shrugged, but fixed her with a penetrating stare. "Sure."

He unfolded his arms and picked up the spoon. "Do you like spaghetti?"

Chapter 13

What did she see in David? Joe punched his pillow and scrunched it up under his head. His back ached from a restless, uncomfortable night on the unyielding, hardwood floor. He couldn't honestly blame his unrest on the sleeping arrangements, but it would be a good excuse. Better to attribute the dull ache inside to the lack of a mattress than to heartache.

What did David have that he didn't have? Okay, besides the obvious two eyes. How could she still think about David after their bout between the sheets? And that amazing seduction on the living room floor that still tantalized him? Thoughts of another woman were impossible after that.

It meant more to him than just scratching an itch. She had fully assaulted his senses, first with her hellcat fire, then with her kittenish softness. He had thought about, yes, even fantasized about her body, her touch, during the years they were apart. She had intrigued him in his imagination but so much more so in reality. Joe had regretted turning his back on her more than a few times. Now he wanted to set things right, make amends. She, apparently, wanted to turn her back on him.

He kicked off the covers, stood up and stretched in an attempt to shake off frustration. The thin blanket around his bare shoulders, the panorama of the park through the windows was a blur.

How could he expect Bobbie to be interested in him more than David or more than any other man? His hand brushed over the eye patch.

Resting his head against the cool glass, he closed his eye. Last night, across the table from her, they had laughed, talked, ate and drank like there had never been anything other than pleasure between them. Natural and fun. It would have been perfect if David weren't an invisible guest at the table, as well.

They had to close this case. All this was too domestic—too distant from the goals. A loner and glad for it, he didn't have room in his life for a relationship. Maybe things weren't perfect, but neither were female entanglements.

He had to keep his priorities straight. Foremost, bring Jimmy's killer to justice. After that, the only thing that meant anything to him was to be active on the force again, working in the field. He couldn't go back to pushing papers. He was in this with Bobbie to achieve those goals, nothing more and nothing less.

The shower started and evoked the mental image of her standing naked and tempting under the hard, pulsing spray. The woman would drive him crazy.

He dropped to the floor and did push ups. After a hundred, a hundred sit ups followed. The exercise helped loosen up muscles, but the running water still tempted him to go get naked with Bobbie.

The phone rang and he checked the caller ID.

"What do you want?" he growled, taking his frustration out on his brother.

"What the hell kind of hello is that?"

"Sorry Brian. What do you have for me?"

****

Bobbie had enjoyed everything about dinner with Joe last night. She hadn't wanted the evening to end, and as long as they refilled their glasses, it didn't.

His stories about growing up with the other Sullivan boys and a solitary sister, more boy than girl, were hilarious. Her heart broke for him when he talked about Jimmy and how much he missed him. They had to find his killer.

The evening would have been a dream come true if she hadn't mentioned David again—a real mood spoiler. No choice. Better to conjure up some self-defense than pretend candlelight and cabernet changed anything.

True, Joe had bewitched her again, made her want him in every way and made it feel mutual. Did he regret slapping her away? Had he buried his unspoken resentment of her? Not sure. Her doubts ran too deep to be glossed over by a tasty dinner and a bowl of gardenias. Last night the old Joe was back: sweet, sometimes self-deprecating, open—and irresistible. It would have been so easy to tell him that she was in love with him, had never stopped. But too much had happened and Joe had changed. He had rejected her after the involvement in her attack resulted in the loss of his eye...and the loss of the old Joe. He rejected her after their lovemaking. The new Joe couldn't be trusted with her heart, so she would somehow have to keep it.

In the shower, a muted sound like a phone ringing spurred Bobbie to turn the water off to hear better. Clearly a phone. She shoved the shower curtain aside, grabbed the plush terry towel off the hook and rushed out of the bathroom wrapping the towel around her.

Joe's outstretched hand silenced her as she hurried in to the living room.

"Great, yeah thanks, Brian. Sure. I'll let you

know."

Her suspicion heightened.

"What?" He struck a pose of pure innocence.

"I heard your phone ring."

"So you had to run out here soaking wet?"

Puddles collected on the floor.

"Oh." He cocked his head. "You figured I'd take off again."

"Understandably."

"I told you I was sorry and I wouldn't do that again. I meant it."

"Mmmhmm." She hitched the towel in a tighter fold over her chest.

"You don't trust me. I guess I wouldn't trust me, either." He laughed.

Then his face froze as he broke eye contact and tracked a cluster of bubbles that slid slowly down her neck, across her chest, and in between her breasts under the towel. The heat of his gaze snaked along her skin as if his hand had followed the bubbles.

His eye was a smoldering, penetrating ember.

Hard to ignore the stirring in her belly but the job should be the only focus. "That was Brian on the phone?"

"Yes." The heat in his stare lowered to simmer as the cool professional kicked in. "Brian has gone through the Safe Choice program records looking for discrepancies and he's talked to officers on desk duty that have been involved in intakes. He thinks records are missing. The numbers in the system between November and Jimmy's death are off. Brian believes the desk guys he spoke to are clean. So he interviewed the guy in charge of the region at the Department of Children and Family Services. Picked up on something that might be significant. One of the DCFS women who's dispatched to pick up Safe Choice babies hasn't been to work in months. Called in to take sick leave. Said she had to have a hysterectomy. May be unrelated, but Brian's going out with a unit to the woman's house now."

Her pulse spiked. "We're close, Joe."

He wiped soap bubbles off her forehead and the simmering between them banked towards boil. His tender touch set off a cascade of sensations from her forehead to the pit of her stomach. She wanted to reach out and take, but remembered that the last time she took charge to get what she wanted, didn't end the way she had hoped.

"Wouldn't want soap in your eye," he whispered, his voice vibrating through her like a caress.

On an exhaled breath she said, "Thank you."

He lowered his head. Their lips met. She melted into the gentle kiss, powerless. Wanting more, she captured his face in her hands and held their lips together.

The towel fell to the floor. Swept against his bare chest, his hands caressing her naked bottom, she sank into the embrace. His erection apparent, she wanted to join with him again, partners in every way.

The shrill sound of the house phone split them apart. He moved to answer it after he cast her a look that rocked her on her feet. It all but screamed that nothing mattered to him more than the job.

She stooped, picked up the towel and wrapped it around her like a shield. She shivered.

He cleared his throat and picked up the receiver.

"Alexander Baron," he drawled. "Great to hear from you, Brad." He stared at her. "Cici and I were just talking about you."

He leaned back against the counter. His crotch still bulged. She sighed and clasped the towel against her breasts.

"Ha ha. Only good things of course, Brad."

He nodded his head. "Great news. Great news. Yes, of course, we can. We'll be there. Appreciate it. Can't wait to tell Cici."

He hung up.

"He has a baby," he said.

She couldn't read his expression. Sadness? Regret? Excitement? Revenge? What made her go against logic where Joe was concerned? They were together only because of her case and his connections—and yet, one look at him and she forgot everything. Nothing else mattered. Only him.

"What time do we have to be there?" she asked.

"Noon. I think we should get there early. Maybe catch him off guard."

He picked his watch up off the end table. "We have plenty of time." He smiled his wicked smile. "Where were we?"

The reversal shook her. All business one minute and all bedroom the next. The job mattered to her, too. "We were going to behave and act like partners," she asserted. "We were going to get back in the shower."

Slowly he reached to untie the string of his maddeningly habitual low-slung sweatpants.

"A shower sounds perfect."

"No way."

"You said we."

"You know what I meant." She dodged as he reached deftly for her towel.

She managed to close the bathroom door and lock it before he could catch up.

He knocked.

"Are you sure you don't want company?"

"I'm sure."

She leaned against the door, glad for the physical barrier between them. They had an apparent truce and that made the job easier—and made life infinitely harder.

What would life be like if they really were about to become a family? Perfect...and just as big a fairy tale as the Barons themselves.

****

The scent of her perfume led Joe to the bedroom. He found her sitting on the bed going through a box of baby clothes. She was a vision dressed in yellow silk, every auburn hair in place, and Cici's signature makeup applied with cover girl precision. He took a moment to enjoy the view before she noticed him leaning against the door jam.

"Look at all the things they sent over. Can you believe how tiny everything is?"

He sat on the bed and picked up a pair of booties. "Hard to believe a human being's feet could start out this small."

"I think I'll bring the yellow outfit and blanket. It'll match Cici's get-up and cover the bases, boy or girl."

"Up to you. I don't have a clue about any of that stuff."

She nodded and set aside the baby clothes. "Do you want children, Joe?"

He squished a colorful, stuffed giraffe with his hand. "There was a time I did. I don't think about it now." He put the toy down. "You want kids?"

"That's all I want."

"What about the FBI? Aren't you one-hundred-percent career?"

"I'd give it up in a minute."

"Really? Then why aren't you married?"

"Guess I haven't found the right man yet," she replied with a shrug.

"That doesn't say much for David. He said you're engaged."

"Did he?" She shook her head. "We aren't. Never were. I guess he wants to be though."

She bent her head over the box of clothes.

He wanted to engulf her in his arms and proclaim his happiness that David posed no threat and had no real claim on her. He could claim her. David didn't deserve her. But neither did he.

He stood up. "Let's go and get us a little baby,

Cici," he drawled.

"Okay, Daddy." She hit him with her most sugary twang. "Let's go."

She popped up and winked at him. "First," Bobbie said, "We need to get my boys in here and get wired up."

She picked up a big, flowery diaper bag that matched her shoes and hooked it over her shoulder. She barked into her phone, tossed it in the bag and then switched gears with her huge, "Cici" eyes. He chuckled following her out the bedroom door and unbuttoned his shirt so the Fibbies could get at him with their equipment.

Chapter 14

Officer Becky Adams watched a limo pull up to the curb in front of her. Concealed behind the screen of smoky glass in Sterling's chauffeured car, Adams observed a couple get out of the limo with mild curiosity. Tall athletic man, slender, ritzy-looking woman—they were a pretty pair.

They laughed and hugged on the Park Avenue sidewalk as if they owned it. *Who knows? Around here maybe they do.*

The limo driver opened the trunk and pulled out a diaper bag and a huge, stuffed teddy bear and handed them to the man. That piqued her attention.

The baby in the car seat next to her snuffled and made strange gurgling sounds causing her to turn toward the infant, alarmed. She lifted the baby from the car seat and held her close to her chest.

Please little one, you need to be quiet. Babies who aren't quiet are taken away and wind up in foster homes. You have a chance at a real home. If only you were a boy. I have enough money put away now. Next boy baby is mine. Then I will disappear and Sterling will never be able to find us. My little Johnny. No one will ever be able to take you away from me again.

Placing the baby back in the car seat, she

stroked the blanket and the squirmy body beneath it until the baby settled down again. The kid had to be delivered in one piece, and then she could forget about it. Twenty grand held in the balance. If Sterling would just call and give her the green light.

Adams peered through the window again and caught a glimpse of the man's profile next to the head of the teddy bear he toted. He looked familiar. She stared at the woman in turn. Red hair. Not that common. The redhead looked familiar, too.

Their backs toward the street as they approached the revolving doors didn't allow her to place them, but she had a feeling about this in her gut. Straining toward the window on full alert now she snatched a fleeting glimpse of the man's face again—chiseled jaw and a scrap of bandage on his eye. The building swallowed them and they were nothing but blurred motion through plate glass.

"Watch the kid a minute," Adams said to the driver. She opened the car door. "I need to check something out. Be right back."

****

Martha greeted Alex and Cici with her unlovely, grim face and ushered them into Sterling's office. Surprised that Sterling wasn't enthroned behind his massive desk, Joe glanced at Bobbie. Her raised eyebrows let him know the surprise was mutual.

"Where's Brad, Martha?" Joe asked.

"Mr. Sterling will be with you in a moment. Can I get you anything?"

"No thank you, pretty lady."

Martha's lips pursed, obviously impervious to Baron's cowboy charm.

"I'm nervous, Daddy."

"Nothing to be nervous about, sugar. Brad brings us our baby and we take the little one home. Right, Martha?"

Martha apparently could care less. She closed the door behind her without a backward glance.

"Not very neighborly," Joe remarked. "I'll have to say something to Brad about that." Joe played to the camera, possibly to Sterling.

He ushered his "wife" toward the leather couch and took a seat next to her. He set the teddy bear down between them and stretched his arm over the stuffed animal and around her shoulder. He swayed her closer to him with a flex of his bicep and smiled at her adoringly. Her pretty, honey-colored eyes glistened with tears. He could see the fierce determination in their depths as he played the role with Cici, but Special Agent Leighton smiled back at him.

Moments later Bradley Sterling entered the office, pompous and self-satisfied. He approached them, hand extended.

Joe rose to take it and gave it a vigorous shake.

"Sorry to keep you waiting," Sterling said. "Today's the day." He clasped both his hands in front of him in an oh-boy pose.

Joe pulled a thick envelope out of his breast pocket and handed it to Sterling. "Thank you for all you did to help us. I want you to know I appreciate it. And I won't forget."

Sterling accepted the envelope without looking at it. "My pleasure."

"Where is the baby? I should say *my* baby. I can hardly believe it." Bobbie pressed a shaky hand to her throat.

"She'll be here any minute."

"She? Our baby is a little girl? Oh, Daddy, did you hear? We have a daughter to love from this day forward." Bobbie turned on the waterworks. Tears rolled, unchecked down her cheeks.

"Cici, honey." Joe squatted down in front of her. "Please don't cry."

Bobbie's crying unsettled Joe even though he knew her emotions were staged. It made him feel guilty, helpless.

"Oh, they're just happy tears," she burbled.

But her eyes were a well of genuine sadness. This meeting, the first crucial step to take Sterling down, was an ending, too—for the Barons, the undercover operation and Bobbie and Joe.

Sterling rounded his desk to answer his phone.

Joe took out a handkerchief and wiped the tears from Bobbie's cheeks.

"I said no interruptions, Martha. Fine, then put it through." Sterling's manner with his secretary was gruff and imperialistic. No wonder the woman never smiled.

The lawyer sat down behind his desk. His manicured fingers tapped impatiently on its mirrored surface.

"I see. I understand. Of course. Yes, I agree. Tomorrow then."

Sterling grabbed Joe's attention at the word, "tomorrow." Their eyes met. Sterling's were blocks of ice. "Yes, handle it," he said into the phone, his lips pulled in a straight line.

Head down, Sterling returned the phone into the receiver with exaggerated care. He picked up the envelope Joe had given to him, circled around the desk and held it out to Joe.

"Bad news to report, I'm afraid."

"What?"

"Your baby will not be here today."

"What's this about? More money? Name your price." Joe pulled a checkbook out of his coat pocket. "Give me the number that will make this happen today."

"It has nothing to do with money. She has a touch of jaundice. They want her to remain an extra day in the hospital nursery under the lights. She should be released tomorrow."

Bobbie burst into tears and sobbed. "We'll never be a family. He's breaking his promise to help us, isn't he?"

"No, darlin', he isn't. We just have to wait one more day. We've waited this long. One more day that's all. Come on, don't cry, Cici."

"I can't stop. Why me? Why can't I have a baby to love?"

"You will, honey, tomorrow. I promise."

He pointed his index finger toward Sterling with an angry thrust. "I never break a promise. I expect you to be true to your word. We will pick up our daughter tomorrow."

While he spoke, Joe sized up Sterling. The man didn't blink, didn't flinch. His eyes were unreadable, dead of any emotion. His gut told him Sterling had made them somehow.

"She will be here tomorrow," Sterling said.

"So will we." Joe picked up the bear, the diaper bag, took Bobbie's hand and led her out of the office. The elevator doors were open. When the doors closed Bobbie buried her head on his chest and sobbed.

"It's okay, honey. Everything will be okay." Joe kept his head bent over Bobbie, hyper-aware of the cameras in each corner of the elevator.

He expected to be faced with at least one unfriendly at the other end of a gun when the doors opened to the lobby, but only a crush of impassive commuters waited for them to exit the elevator. They made it back to the limo unimpeded.

Joe helped Bobbie into the car and moved to the other side, sweeping his eye to take in as much around him as he could. He didn't detect a tail during the brief, limited survey.

He slid in next to Bobbie and slammed the door.

"He made us in there," Joe said.

"Yeah, he did. It was the call. Somebody probably made us on our way into the building."

"I thought of that, too. If there's a Chicago connection, I might have been recognized."

"Doesn't matter," Bobbie said dryly. "It's over. There won't be a tomorrow. We do have him taking the money and talking about delivery of a baby, though."

"He gave the money back."

"Yeah, but no baby, here's your bucks. Still establishes the delivery of a baby required the payment in the first place."

Joe took off the cowboy hat and dragged his fingers through his hair with a frustrated swipe. "We have to wait and see what Brian finds at the DCFS woman's house. We still have a case to build. But the Barons are useless now."

"Right. We can both go home. I think I'll move out tonight."

That well of sadness reflected in her eyes again. Nothing he could do about it since he belonged in Chicago and she lived here. He itched to get with Brian and move the investigation right back to Bradley Sterling's Park Avenue address as soon as they could, looking forward to using his skills again, even if the undercover operation was a bust.

"When we get back I'll check flights," he said. "Probably won't get anything out until morning, though."

"Fine."

The car glided along city streets. John had become an expert in circumventing traffic. Joe figured the kid poured over maps and checked traffic patterns on the Internet to impress his commanding officer.

"If you don't mind, John..." Bobbie leaned forward and met Donaldson's eyes in the rear view mirror. "I'd like to stop and pick up some groceries. Two blocks down, on the left. If we're being tailed, no reason to not look normal."

She leaned back. "Let me make dinner tonight and pay you back for the meal you made last night, okay? I can leave in the morning, too."

"Sure."

He didn't know how to interpret her vibes.

Tension strained between them again. He wanted to banish it. He wanted her...to kiss him like she did this morning, to bed him like she did a few days ago, to cook for him, to eat what he cooked, to run around in nothing but a towel. He wanted her to stay with him—in a penthouse or in a tent.

The car slowed, then stopped. She crawled over his lap to get out his side. On the sidewalk she leaned back in. "I'll see you at home, Daddy." She grinned.

"Wait," Joe said. "Donaldson, hand me my gun."

The agent opened the glove box and passed back a Glock. Joe waved Bobbie in closer to him.

"Here. Take this with you."

She focused on the gun. "I didn't know you had this on you."

"I didn't. It's been in the car." He wrapped her hand around the cold metal. "I don't think we're being tailed. Take it anyway."

She nodded. "All right. Thanks."

She advised Donaldson, "I'll grab a cab when I'm done, John." "I'll be back in an hour or so," she told Joe. "If not, send the team."

Chapter 15

Bobbie's narrow, four-inch high heel tilted sideways and her right ankle twisted painfully. Her feet were killing her and she longed to slip into sneakers or any blessedly flat shoe. She minced into the crowded city market.

She maneuvered her cart through the congested aisles, sufficiently balanced by hanging on to it, so her feet didn't distract her from thinking about the depressing turn in her meticulous case against Sterling. How had they been made?

It had to be Joe. Someone recognized him. The Sullivan family was well known in the greater Chicago police community and had been for decades. John Sullivan's tenure as Commissioner had him in the public eye for years. Danny had been decorated for heroism more than once. And Joe, himself, had been highly visible when he caught the Henna Housewife Killer. A bandage, an eye patch, what did it matter? For weeks afterward his bandaged face had been the lead news image in the media.

How stupid that he had figured in the UC operation. It was bound to fail from the start. Tears of frustration pooled in her eyes. She swiped them away, angry with her superiors, herself and the world in general.

What bothered her more, the dismal state of her case or the fact that there was no longer any reason for Joe to stay in New York? How could she survive losing him again?

She should still be furious with him for manipulating and scheming his way into her case only to wreck it. Instead, she longed for him to continue manipulating his way into her life.

But he would go and she already mourned his loss. How could she go back to the way things were before this case?

She forced herself to concentrate on grocery selection. Normally, this was one of her favorite places—grocery shopping was one of her favorite things to do. She loved to cook, loved every part of meal assembly.

She tossed a few things in her cart and eyed the glistening display of seafood on ice: plump shrimp, lobster tails, pastel salmon, and thick tuna fillets. The smell of the yeasty breads made her stomach grumble pleasantly.

On a day long ago in Chicago she had lovingly chose the ingredients of a gourmet feast to prepare for Joe. All those ingredients were flung around a parking lot during the vicious attack. She had never made that meal for Joe, never had revealed that she loved him then.

She pressed her hand on her midriff. The lovemaking. She had no idea back then what they could be together, where they could take each other. And still she had mourned his loss and suffered from his rejection.

How do I survive the pain again after making love with Joe?

In the checkout line she stood, her mind reeling. She peered at the items assembled in the metal basket, as if taking stock. She reached down along her sides, took off each shoe and threw them in the cart.

She left the market in her stocking feet.

****

Donaldson had barely braked at the curb when Joe shoved out of the car and slammed the door behind him.

The doorman held the door open for him. "Good afternoon, Mr. Baron."

Joe stalked into the lobby without acknowledging the man, too aggravated to be civil, let alone graciously southern.

He stomped into the apartment after virtually ignoring the attendant in the elevator, banged the door closed, half off its hinges, and reached a hand under his shirt. He clawed the strips of tape off his torso taking hunks of chest hair with them and tossed the wire across the room.

He wanted to break something, punch the wall, anything to relieve the frustration, the impotence. What the hell happened? He had to know who had fingered them. *Damn it to hell.*

They had Sterling on tape setting up the baby drop, but no way would the charges stick. Now positive that Sterling was responsible for Jimmy's death, he had to find a way to nail him for it. He needed to find out who had called Sterling.

Joe dialed Brian's number and paced.

The connection clicked. He didn't wait for a greeting.

"Someone made us," Joe spat out. He punched his hand against the wall, relishing the pain that shot up his arm.

"How?"

"How the hell should I know?" he yelled.

"Take it easy. I didn't give you up."

"Okay. Okay. I know." He leaned his head against the wall. "Sorry, Bri. I'm fucking nowhere with this."

"That makes two of us."

"You didn't question the DCFS woman?"

"She's gone. No sign of her at her house. No evidence of forced entry. Suitcase in the closet, nothing apparently missing. Zip."

"Shit. I need something, Brian."

"We have an APB out. We're questioning co-workers, rounding up relatives. Not much else we can do."

Joe nodded. "We were so close. Sterling received a phone call while we were there and in a split second everything fell apart. It has to be someone from Chicago."

"You could be right. Then you were the one that got made."

"Probably." Dread dove in Joe's belly thinking about Bobbie's face in the car. "Bobbie hates my guts. She's bound to blame me for blowing her case. She'll never forgive me."

The doorknocker sounded.

"Here she is now. Time to face the music. She stopped for groceries for dinner, probably something with a side of poison. Hold on."

Joe put the phone down on the coffee table to have his hands free to help her with the bags. He went to the door, his stomach muscles tense, dreading facing the accusation in Bobbie's eyes.

He swung the door open and faced the business end of a gun.

"Hands up where I can see them and back up real slow," the woman said.

Joe raised his hands over his head and backed a few feet away from her.

She kept the gun trained on his head, crossed the threshold and closed the door behind her. She waved the pistol toward the dining room table. "Over there. Sit down."

Joe obeyed and prayed that the phone was in range and Brian had already called for back up.

Her hand trembled on the gun.

"Don't shoot," he said calmly. "What do you want? Money? There's an envelope of cash in my coat pocket. Take it. It's all yours."

Sure he'd seen her before, Joe tried to place the face.

She grimaced. "I don't want your money, asshole. You Sullivan boys are all alike, aren't you? Jimmy was an asshole, too. Runs in the family."

Joe froze at the mention of his brother's name.

The gun trained on his head pointed to the floor and then up again. "Down on your knees, Sullivan."

****

"Down on your knees, Sullivan."

Jimmy complied, nice and easy. I keep my distance. He could spring up and I can't have that.

"It doesn't have to go down this way, Becky. Let me take you in. If you give up Sterling, I can work a deal for you."

I almost split my side laughing, but I keep the gun pointed dead center on his forehead. "That's rich, Sullivan. You're so important—all the Sullivans get the glory. Here's the deal. Beg and maybe I won't kill you."

"Fuck you, bitch."

****

"I said down on your knees, Sullivan."

Joe lunged at her, but she shoved the gun into his forehead with ample force to ram him against the back of the chair.

"I'll shoot you if you make another move," she sneered.

"Go ahead." He sat for the moment and glared at her. "What are you waiting for?"

"Your lovely wife Cici, of course."

"Why?"

"Why? How stupid are you?"

He recognized her now. She had been at his brother's funeral, in uniform. When she had expressed her condolences to him then, she had the same predatory, malicious gleam in her eyes as she did now.

"Very stupid, apparently. Educate me," he said.

"We have a good thing going here. Your brother tried to shut it down and failed. I even offered him a cut of the action. But not Mr. Squeaky Clean. He wouldn't accept the offer. Too greedy for the glory. He should have joined forces with Sterling instead of threatening him."

"What do you mean join forces?" *Brian better be getting all of this on tape.* He had to keep her talking. He might get shot when he made his move on her, but with any luck Sterling would be brought down first.

"Sterling sets up the fat cats with the big bucks. They buy a baby. We get a big payday. Everyone wins and no one gets hurt. That is, until your brother tried to play me. No one wants these babies anyway. They throw them away like garbage. The foster care system? What a fucking joke. Kids disappear into that hellhole. I know. We are doing a service here."

"Why did you kill my brother?"

"I just told you. Mr. Sterling doesn't like any loose ends. Neither do I. Jimmy was a loose end. He wouldn't let it go. He pissed me off. I had no choice."

"Everyone has a choice."

"We wanted him silenced. He's silenced. He was a thorn in everybody's side."

"Are you saying that Sterling ordered my brother's death?"

"Are you slow? Isn't that what I just said? Sterling told me to handle it. I handled it. Glad to do it. Jimmy needed to be gone."

Sterling would go down no matter what happened now. His muscles bunched and adrenaline flowed as he weighed how he would engineer the rest of this. "It doesn't have to go like this," he said. "Tell the cops what you know about Sterling and it might buy you some leniency."

She laughed.

"Go like what? Who's holding the gun, asshole? Tell the cops. That's a good one. They already know."

Bile rose in his throat. "Who's in this with you?"

"You'd be surprised."

"Nothing surprises me anymore."

"No? How about McClellan, Thompson or Allegro?"

"Allegro? He's been on the force thirty years. He's known my family my whole life. No way is he dirty."

"Really? Like I said, you would be surprised. You Sullivans think everybody's as greedy for glory as you are."

****

Bobbie sat in the back of the cab and stared vacantly out the smeared window. She massaged a foot to warm it after walking on cold concrete.

Tonight she would be back home, back to her normal routine, back to David and trying to please her father. And missing Joe all over again.

It seemed like she had spent her whole life loving Joe then missing him. Trying to forget about him. Trying to live her life without him. She would make a clean break tonight, wouldn't wait until tomorrow.

Did she want to stay the night knowing what could and most likely would happen between them?

Be honest. Yes, she wanted to make love with him one more time, something to savor in the future. He ruined everything by forcing himself into this case. She should hate him but she didn't and never could. She loved him.

The cab pulled up in front of her building. She paid the driver and half-hopped to the door. Her feet stung from the frigid sidewalk as if she were stepping on hot coals.

"Mrs. Baron? Where are your shoes?" The

doorman hovered over her after his rush to meet her, his brows pinched with concern. "Were you accosted, madam?"

"No, nothing like that, you sweet man." She drawled, one last time as Cici. "I gave them away...to someone who needed them more than me."

"Yes, ma'am. Very generous." His face relaxed, then bloomed in a smile. "You'll want to hurry upstairs for the surprise."

What the hell is he babbling about? Had she slipped up and forgotten something?

"I'm in on the secret," he continued. "His sister told me all about it. She said it's a surprise."

"Whose sister?"

"Mr. B's. She arrived a few minutes ago. She told me all about the birthday party, so I let her up."

Bobbie whipped out her phone. "Need assistance," she shouted into the mouthpiece without a trace of southern accent, "Penthouse floor."

She whirled on the doormen and flashed her badge. "Do not let anyone leave this building. Go through your emergency protocol if you like. FBI is on the way."

Gun in hand, she raced to the elevator and waved the startled attendant out. The elevator reached the top floor and she crouched, gun cocked against the edge of one of the doors as it opened. Finding the outer hall clear, she rushed to the penthouse door and pressed her ear against it. A female voice and then the rumble of a deep voice.

Thank you God.

She closed her eyes, took a cleansing breath and turned the knob soundlessly, her heart pounding in her chest. She pushed the door open inch-by-inch, gun raised. A woman faced Joe with a gun pointed at his head.

"FBI. Drop the gun!"

The woman swiveled, eyes wide, and with a

menacing sneer her gun arm whipped around in Bobbie's direction. Joe lunged at the woman from behind. They plunged forward and the woman's gun discharged.

As glass shattered overhead, Bobbie fired a direct hit between the woman's eyes. Bone fragments and brain matter splattered the walls, the carpet and Joe as he landed on top of the woman.

He disengaged from the woman's corpse and stood up inches from where the body sprawled.

"Great shot, Sullivan," Bobbie said.

His brows knit as she pitched his gun over to him.

He caught it and stared at her. "What the...?"

His face rigid and pale, freckled with blood, he wiped it with his hand and smeared maroon streaks across one cheek.

A finger to her lips, she hitched her silk blouse up to reveal the wire still taped in place. His face vacant, he nodded.

He understands. She dusted glass shards off her shoulders with a steady hand while her insides shook in spasms.

His eye bored a hole in her as he picked his cell phone up off the coffee table.

"Brian, are you still there?"

****

"Thank God. Jesus, Joe, what happened?"

"She's dead. You heard everything?"

Joe's legs shook and finally gave way. He sank down on the couch.

"Yeah, I heard. Got it on tape."

"Thank you. We have all we need now to put Sterling away," Joe said. He stared at Bobbie. She hadn't moved from the spot since she came into the place.

"I alerted Uncle Frankie. I want to talk to him when he gets there," Brian said.

"No problem. I'm sure he'll want to talk to you,

too. Hold on okay."

"Hey, bro?"

"Yeah?"

"Thanks for calling."

Joe laughed. Bobbie looked at him as if he were crazy. "You're welcome, Bri."

Bobbie faced John Donaldson when he burst through the door. "You got here fast, Donaldson. Good work."

"I was still listening to the wire, ma'am. From before the operation went south..." Joe could swear the guy blushed in Bobbie's presence.

"As soon as you called for back up, I double-parked the car and sprinted ten blocks to get here."

Bobbie smiled and patted the rookie's arm. "Great job. Thanks, John, for watching my back."

Donaldson beamed. Then law enforcement personnel swarmed the place. It looked to Joe like the entire New York police force and the East Coast contingent of smug FBI agents squeezed into the apartment, man for man.

Bobbie came over to him. "Brian recorded this?"

"Yeah. I was on the phone with him when she came in. I unlocked the door. I thought it was you."

Joe shook his head remembering the stupid move. "Brian has it on tape," he said. "Sterling ordered her to kill Jimmy, and us, after she made me. He's going down. This is big. She gave up some other cops. We nailed him, Bobcat."

She flinched. "She was a cop?"

"Yes. I thought she looked familiar. I couldn't place her, but then it clicked. She killed Jimmy and had the stones to show up at his funeral. Can you believe that? I remember seeing her there."

Frank Monahan marched into the room. The Fibbies present fell silent. Bobbie acknowledged her boss on a bead toward Joe, with a clipped, "Sir." She stepped away from the couch and cast Joe a look of outrage.

"Brian called him," Joe said as he stood to shake Monahan's outstretched hand.

"Great job, Joe," Uncle Frankie said.

Joe accepted the handshake and gauged Bobbie's reactions over Monahan's shoulder. "Thanks, Uncle Frankie."

"Your dad will be proud."

"I didn't do it alone. Leighton..."

"Just like a Sullivan not to want any of the glory. You're a good man, Joe. You deserve to be back on the force. I'll make a few calls on your behalf when I get back to my office. I will make it happen."

Bobbie stood aside as he accepted the congratulations, her eyes wide and her face expressionless.

"Bobbie was the one—"

She cut Joe off. "I'd like to make my statement now, if I might, sir." She stepped in between the two men, her back to Joe. "If you wouldn't mind coming with me to the other room, sir? I have some notes I'd like to refer to."

"Sure." Monahan clamped a hand on Joe's shoulder. "Again, good work."

****

Bobbie would end this her way. After she had submitted her version of a statement, she saw Monahan to the door and slipped into the bedroom, avoiding contact with Joe.

After changing into comfortable jeans and a sweater and doing some haphazard packing, her suitcase bulged. She only took the personal things she had brought with her and left the expensive wardrobe in the closet, forever leaving Cici Baron behind with it.

One last glance around the room. The diamond hearts necklace lay on her bedside table. She picked it up, traced the two hearts with her finger, fastened the chain and tucked it inside her sweater. The trinket would serve as a reminder of her time spent with Joe.

Bobbie left the heavy luggage in the hallway. In the living room Joe still sat on the couch talking on the phone. The ME had removed the body already. The sight of the bloodstain on the carpet gave her another bout of shivers.

Joe noticed her standing there, glanced at the suitcase on the floor behind her and snapped the phone shut. He stood and crossed the room. "You're leaving now? Didn't we agree on tomorrow?"

"It's over."

"Bobbie..." He held an upturned palm toward her, his face crestfallen.

Her throat tightened.

"We're even now." She turned away from him.

A grab for her suitcase and she hurried out of the Baron penthouse, out of his life again.

Chapter 16

Special Agent Roberta Leighton wanted to be back to work, returned to her satisfying life without Joe Sullivan, round two. She sat at her desk again, her calendar full—but life was far from what she wanted.

She shoved papers around and pushed her morning coffee away. The smell disgusted her. She had lost her taste for it and most everything else.

The small pleasures she had enjoyed before: fixing a great meal, pushing her muscles to the limit at the gym, jogging in the predawn hours, quiet conversations with David, did nothing to soothe the constant ache from turning her back on Joe.

Hollow, exhausted and stifled, she had to psyche herself up to get out of bed every day to tackle the daily routines that she had savored before her stint as Cici Baron.

The Sterling file grew thicker by the day. She had had the pleasure of apprehending Bradley Sterling and that memory bolstered her spirits some. It had been wonderful to witness his slick veneer crumble under the weight of the charges against him. Martha had even winked at her as Bobbie led her boss out the door in cuffs with Donaldson proud at her side—his first collar.

She had no regrets that she had tampered with the facts in her report of the shooting incident at the penthouse. Yes, she shot Becky Adams, not Joe. It didn't matter to her. His report had contradicted hers, of course, and she had been vehemently questioned about the conflicting statements.

Internal investigators ascertained the need for the use of deadly force through Brian's tape, so they both were in the clear on that, and she didn't care that her statement appeared suspicious. Joe's gun fired the shot, and she believed as long as she held fast that Joe pulled the trigger, he would be returned to active duty.

He deserved it. Clearly that's all he had wanted from her. She could give it to him despite the persistent pain his rejection of what she most wanted to give him caused her.

She had no regrets that she had refused contact with Joe. She had delegated any collaboration between Chicago homicide and her agency on the Sterling case to Special Agent Donaldson.

A quote by Joyce Carol Oates played in her mind like an anthem. "Revenge is living well, without you." She had lived well, would live well again without Joe. How long would it take? She had already spent two miserable months and feared her malaise would drag out for years if she didn't do something, anything to wipe the slate clean and get on with it, damn it.

She shoved up from her desk with the intention of pounding out her ever-present frustrations on the treadmill in the office gym. She passed Donaldson who always had that shiny, new penny look on his face since she had commended his work on the Sterling op.

"Hey, John."

"Good morning, ma'am." He stopped in his tracks, stiffened with formality, although he still wore that shiny penny smile.

She laughed and touched his sleeve. "For the umpteenth time, you can call me Bob..." Her head spun and her peripheral vision blurred. Her ears hummed as she teetered sideways.

Strong hands clamped around the sides of her arms and held her upright. She closed her eyes until the buzzing subsided and the dizzy swirls abated. She blinked her eyes open. John's face confronted her.

The vibes of hero worship for her that he usually emitted were replaced by concern. "Are you okay?"

"Sure." She gave him a weak smile. "I skipped breakfast. Must have caught up with me."

"You know what? You don't look okay," he said. "Maybe you better sit down." His hands still held her steady.

"No, I'm good. You can let me go now."

His eyes held hers for a second, then flashed, embarrassed. He dropped his hands. "Yes, ma'am."

She shook her head, amused. "John, I order you to call me Bobbie." Her stomach constricted and her smile faded. She clutched a hand at her midriff.

"I must have a touch of the flu or something. I think I will sit down."

"Sure, ma'am...Bobbie... over here."

Her head spun again. She closed her eyes, which made her feel even more off-balance and she swayed. John's hands steadied her again, this time steering her to a chair.

"Put your head down."

He applied gentle pressure on the back of her neck. His spicy aftershave made her stomach heave.

"I think I better go home," she said, looking at the floor. "Cover my desk for me?"

"Sure. Can I call someone?"

She raised her head with effort.

"To get you home?"

"David," she said thickly. "David Harper. His

number is in my book. Could you please ask him to send over the company car? I don't feel like dealing with the subway."

She slumped in the chair and massaged the back of her neck. John appeared a few minutes later with a glass of water in hand. She accepted it and wet her lips.

"Car's on the way," John said.

"Thanks." She handed back the cup, down just a couple sips. "I'll head outside. See you tomorrow. You can call me if you need anything."

"I can handle everything. Get some rest. Maybe get checked at the doctor."

John smiled and she saw him in a new light. The look of hero worship she gave *him* made him blush.

****

Bobbie felt marginally better outside. Sunlight versus florescent light, she turned her face upward, eyes closed, to soak up some vitamin D. But the air she breathed on the clogged city street could hardly be called "fresh."

Minutes later her father's company car braked at the curb. She glanced through the window, surprised to see David at the wheel.

"I thought you'd send the driver." Bobbie slid into the passenger seat of the Lincoln but barely had the strength to close the door.

David's stony face made her stomach fall with dread, adding to the overall nausea that rolled inside her.

"I was worried about you." He glanced her way and then focused on the traffic.

She rubbed her arms to warm them. So cold, yet covered with a film of perspiration. She shivered and cupped her forehead in her hand. "I must have a fever."

"Want me to stop at Doctor Baker's office? I'll bully him into seeing you as a walk-in."

"No. Thanks." She touched his sleeve. "I just want to go to bed."

"Okay. Close your eyes and rest a little. I'll get you there."

She just made it into her bathroom before she lost what little liquid she had taken in earlier. Quaking, she anchored herself by clasping each hand wide over the sink top. She dampened a washcloth and pressed it to her temple.

Her face was so white in the mirror that the splash of freckles over the bridge of her nose seemed black. She opened the medicine cabinet, pulled out a bottle of mouthwash and rinsed away some of the sour taste.

Draping the damp cloth around her neck, she went to find David.

He sat, hunched forward, elbows on his thighs, on one of the living room chairs. Her approach snapped his head up and he assessed her coolly.

"You look a little better now."

She sank down on the couch. "I feel a little better, thanks. Hope it lasts. This is the pits. You were right. I should have gotten that flu shot."

He squinted at her, the silence between them palpable, like a shimmering wall that separated them. Her mantle clock ticked, the heat fan clicked and whirred. Seconds in this limbo of disengagement hung like hours. If he'd only leave, she could crawl into bed, close her eyes and shut out everything.

"I don't want to keep you from work. I'll be fine," she said.

"I'm not ready to leave. Not without having my say."

"David, please. I'm just not up to conversation right now. Maybe tonight? I'll make you dinner." Her stomach pitched and she grimaced.

"Huh." He folded his arms over his chest and sat back, bemused. "I'm not looking for conversation. You don't have to say a word."

He leaned forward and glared. "You've put me off since that whole undercover thing with the cowboy..."

She sighed, exasperated. "Give me a break, David. I've been sick. I just can't get rid of this bug I caught and I promise—"

"Be quiet, Roberta. I mean it."

She shut up, stunned at his forcefulness. He could be stiff, formal, and sometimes even prissy. But she had never seen him act so emphatic.

"You want nothing to do with me. You slap me away at every turn," he asserted.

"That's not true."

"No? When's the last time we made love?"

"Uh..." Her mind raced. "It was..."

"I'll tell you." He stood up. "I can't remember, either."

She pulled the washcloth off her neck and tossed it on the coffee table. "We've both been busy and I've been sick—"

"You're sick all right. You're lovesick."

"What do you mean?"

"What do you think I'm blind?" He thrust his head back and looked at the ceiling. Then he leveled his gaze at her.

"Roberta, this isn't working. We don't work."

"Oh, David. That's not true. I care for you very, very much."

"I believe you do. But it's not enough."

"David, please. Please don't do this now."

He sat down next to her and clasped her hands in his. "Look."

She fastened her eyes on his face.

"No matter what you think, this has never been about romancing the boss's daughter for me."

"I know that." She sighed.

"But." He tightened his hands. "For you, it's been about keeping Daddy happy."

"You can't be serious." She frowned at him.

"I'm dead serious." He let her hands drop. "I want more, Roberta. I want a wife, children."

"I want that, too," she said meekly.

"Not as much as you want your job. Your undercover ops, your merit badges...your cowboy." He stood and paced in front of her.

She shook her head. "That's not true, either." Tears welled and stung the corners of her eyes. "The job isn't everything. And he isn't *my* cowboy," she whispered.

The pacing stopped. His lips tight, his eyes fierce with intent, he said, "Maybe. But it's over. We're over."

She rose, her heart hammering. "All right," she said softly.

He looked at the floor. When he faced her again the fire in his eyes had extinguished. His chest expanded and his jaw rolled as if to contain the flood of hurt.

She could hardly bear that she had caused him pain. Nostalgia weakened her, almost made her retract her agreement to end their relationship. Who knew better than she about wanting someone and not being wanted back?

"I'm sorry, David. I never meant to hurt you." Tears streamed down her face.

He folded his arms over his middle, squeezed his eyes shut a moment, and opened them to gaze at her face. A glimmer of a smile played on his lips. "You have nothing to be sorry for. You never misled me. I've done a lot of thinking lately. I'm the one who made this more than it is."

He picked up his jacket from the arm of the chair. "We had a nice time together, Roberta. Let's leave it at that."

She moved around the coffee table and stepped into his arms, her chin on his shoulder. His hug was warm, familiar—the arms of a friend. Easy to forget heartache in the temporary comfort of David's embrace.

He loosened his hold and took a step away from her. "I have to get back to work."

"Okay."

At the door he turned back toward her and smiled. "I'll take care of keeping Daddy happy."

His smile was contagious.

In the hall David's resolute expression hurt her. "Take care, Roberta."

"You, too." *I should do something, say something.*

"Do me a favor?" he asked, a wry expression on his face.

"Anything," she agreed, hopeful at the opportunity.

"If you have a boy, don't tell me about it."

Chapter 17

"Oh my god!" Molly whooped.

Her dear friend's delighted face welcomed Bobbie. But the waft of pine air freshener that drifted through Molly's open door was an unwelcome assault to her ultra-sensitive stomach. Bobbie gulped and couldn't offer Molly more than a shaky smile.

"Why didn't you call me? I would have come to the airport to meet you," Molly asserted. "Oh." She fixed on a point over Bobbie's shoulder. "That's your car, isn't it?"

"Yes. I drove." Bobbie glanced at her Toyota. Bug splatter covered the windshield and sandy mud-sprays fanned out over the wheel wells. The stuffed back seat held clothes on hangers and dog-eared boxes, from the floor to the moon roof.

"You drove from New York?" Molly stared at the car, puzzled. "Are you moving back home?"

Bobbie glanced away from the car and faced Molly. Her friend, the only woman in the world who Bobbie considered family, was the picture of delight at the prospect that her prodigal "sister" had returned.

"Uh..." Bobbie shifted on her feet and shrugged,

helpless to explain further.

"Come in, come in." Molly grabbed her hand and pulled her forward.

Bobbie stepped into the hallway and the years rewound, back to when it had been her job and her joy to scrub the shiny floors under her feet to a satiny sheen. For a moment it was as if she had never left. Until Amy appeared at the top of the stairs—her little Amy—with hips and breasts. And were those car keys dangling in her hand?

"Bobbie!" Amy galloped down the stairs and Bobbie had a flashback of the little girl, ponytail flying behind her, instead of the young woman with the mass of raven curls and makeup on her face.

Amy threw her arms around Bobbie and hugged tight. "Want to go for a ride? Momma and Daddy bought me a car for my birthday. It's sweeeet. And a hybrid. Eco-friendly. That's so important. Come on..." Amy tugged, playful, at Bobbie's hand.

"Bobbie's tired, sweetie," Molly slung an arm over Amy's shoulder. "You go on. Maybe Bobbie will be up for a ride later."

"Yes?"

"I'd love to," Bobbie said.

"Okay. Bye." Amy smacked a kiss on Bobbie's cheek, then her mother's and breezed out the door.

Molly closed the door behind Amy, turned and leaned against it. She assessed Bobbie, her keen expression diagnosing Bobbie as surely as if she were sitting on Molly's examining table.

"Daddy?" Bobbie asked.

Molly smiled. "That's what she calls Danny."

Bobbie smiled back at her. "That's wonderful, Mol."

"It is." Molly's eyes bored into her. "The kids are over at Kay's until dinner, so we have the house to ourselves. How about I get you a glass of wine? Or maybe a glass of milk?"

Bobbie's stomach turned and she didn't catch

Molly's pointed insinuation. "Mind if I use your rest room? It's been a while since my last pit stop."

"Sure." Molly pushed away from the door. "I'll be in the kitchen."

Bobbie hastened to close the powder room door and muffle the sounds of getting sick yet again. Once her stomach had emptied, she experienced some relief. She splashed water on her face and swigged from the large bottle of mouthwash she perpetually lugged around in her purse. As composed as she could manage, she left the bathroom and plodded into Molly's kitchen. An aura of *Scope* clung to her— her perfume *du jour* lately.

She joined Molly at the kitchen table and accepted the box of saltines that Molly wordlessly slid in her direction with a poignant look. Bobbie opened the box and took out a cracker, head bent to the simple task. She nibbled on the end of the saltine, and held one hand beneath the other to catch crumbs, reluctant to meet Molly's eyes.

"So." Molly said. "I'd say November. Maybe before Thanksgiving?"

Bobbie raised her head. Molly, ever the doctor, had nailed her due date.

"How did you know?"

Molly shot her a "duh" stare. "You mean before I took in your pale face, your penchant to hold one hand over your abdomen, your frequent swallowing, the hormonal flush—or after you puked in the bathroom?"

"You mean I don't glow?" Bobbie laughed.

Molly clasped both Bobbie's hands and laughed with her. "Well, the cold sweat that preceded your trip to the bathroom did reflect some light."

"Why do they call it *morning* sickness anyway?" Bobbie bit into the cracker. "It's almost five in the afternoon for godsakes."

"I was sick all the time with Joey and I wasn't with either of the girls. Maybe you're having a boy."

A strange envy pinched at Bobbie hearing Molly's son's name, Joe's namesake in the Sullivan family. If a boy, her baby might have been named for Joe, too.

Molly's expression turned serious. "Are you and David married now?"

"No," Bobbie blurted overly loud. "No, we're not," she said more softly.

"I guess that was a stupid question. It looks like your car's packed. Did you leave him?"

"Yes. A few weeks ago."

"Does he know about the baby?"

"He seems to. But it doesn't concern him. He's not the father."

"What do you mean he's not the father? Honey, we have been *so* out of touch."

Bobbie sucked in a breath and stared through the bay window at the shady yard. The plantings were still largely dormant, but some tender green buds and shoots made their April entrance in Molly's garden. The familiar vista didn't have the peaceful, now-you're-home effect on her she had hoped it would when she set out on her road trip to Chicago. She felt more bereft and displaced than ever.

Bobbie hadn't really thought anything through since the home pregnancy test had turned out positive. The only course of action that had occurred to her, while she sat on the toilet lid and stared at the + sign on a stick, was to follow her heart. Foremost, she knew in her heart that she wanted the baby. Already the unborn child *was* her heart.

Next, her heart led her here to Molly. If the adage about home and heart applied at all, then this house, Molly's house, was as close as Bobbie had ever come to her idea of home.

She had to tell Molly the truth. Wasn't that the reason she came? She needed to confide in someone, and her only someone was Joe's sister-in-law, a sad truth. She trusted Molly absolutely, but she still panicked at the brink of the admission. What would happen to her if Joe somehow found out?

She didn't know which would terrify her more: his rejection of her *and* their baby or his acknowledgement of them out of honor, instead of love. She couldn't bear either outcome. He could never find out.

"I don't want the father to know about the baby. Not *ever*," Bobbie asserted.

"Honey, is that wise? Was this some kind of a fling? A one-night thing?"

Molly's expression was loving, not at all judgmental.

Bobbie appreciated the implied acceptance—and the irony. "Yeah. The whole thing spanned less than twelve hours." She chuckled. "If you don't count the years of imagining what the one night might be like. Joe's the father of my child," she said.

A myriad of expressions played across Molly's face: incredulous, joyful, quizzical, troubled and conflicted. *She can say a lot of things to me after that bombshell. How is this possible? You and Joe were lovers? Why didn't you tell me? Why didn't he tell me? Do you love him? Does he love you? You can't keep this from him. He'd want to know...*

"How can I help you?" Molly asked, belying Bobbie's thoughts.

Gratitude swamped Bobbie. She burst into tears. Molly's arms enfolded her as if to meld with her, and the fledgling life inside her, to stand with them against the world.

"Don't cry, sweetie. You're not alone. I'll do anything you want to help you and your baby. It will be okay."

It will. Bobbie had to believe that. She gradually stopped crying. "I promise you I *will win* over these hormones and not bawl every five minutes."

Molly set her loose and sat back in her chair.

Bobbie met her eyes, intelligent, loving, capable

Molly. "I could use a good doctor." She smiled.

"I'll write you a script for pre-natal vitamins. Did you see an OB in New York?"

"No. I went to my primary care doctor for a blood test. Just to confirm the home pregnancy test. After that, all I did was resign and pack."

"Surely you don't have to give up your career, sweetie. Why did you resign? Couldn't you take a leave of absence instead?"

"I could. But I don't want to. It's bad enough this baby will have one parent. I know what that's like. The job's too dangerous."

"But you love it, don't you?"

"Sure. But I already love my child more. No contest."

"Are you planning to stay in Chicago permanently? What about your father? Don't you want to raise the baby near your family?"

Bobbie snorted. "Dad and I aren't much of a family, Mol. I could use a place to stay... just until I can buy a place of my own. I have my trust fund and income from my mother's business. I don't need to work."

Bobbie's resolution to conquer her hormones wilted and she dissolved in tears again. "I didn't know where else to go. I don't know what to do."

She put her head down on the table and cried. She wanted to stay there with her inflamed cheek against the cool, wood surface and not move, not think beyond how good it felt to have Molly's hand rub gentle circles on her back.

"Let's think this through. Sit up, Bobbie. No more crying," Molly coaxed her gently.

She lifted her head and mopped her face with the napkin Molly stuffed in her hand.

"Of course you could stay here, but there's the significant problem of my husband. I'd have to lie to him and I won't do that."

"Of course not. I'd never ask you to."

"And trust me, my kids have big mouths, too."

"I didn't think of that."

"Even if I could get Danny to swear not to tell Joe, and that's a huge *if,* how could you hide your pregnancy from Joe? He's over here all the time."

Frustrated tears welled. She needed Molly, wanted to live near her, but she had to step back into the Sullivan-saturated world in Chicago to do it.

"This is hopeless, isn't it, Mol?" She stared at her best friend, tears streaming. "I wouldn't even get to see you. I don't know what I was thinking."

"Are you sure you don't want to tell Joe about the baby?"

Bobbie shut her eyes and shook her head. That much she *had* thought through. If Joe had wanted her he would have never let her leave Chicago in the first place. If he had wanted her after they had unwittingly made this baby together, he wouldn't have pushed her away. If he had wanted her after she left him at the penthouse, he would have come after her.

What Joe wanted didn't include her, much less a baby.

"I'll go back to New York, Molly. This isn't going to work."

Molly cast her a heartbroken look. "I don't want you to go." Her eyes widened. "I have an idea. Why don't you stay downtown in our condo?"

"What condo?"

"Danny sold his condo when we were married and we bought a one bedroom on LaSalle overlooking the river. It's a great place. We rarely stay there anymore. It's small but would be perfect for you."

"What if Danny wants to go there? I don't want to put you in an awkward position."

"We've been talking about remodeling it for a couple years. I'll tell him I'm working on it and it's all torn up. He won't question that. And I'll have an excuse to come and visit you whenever I can. What do you think?"

Bobbie warmed to the idea. "I love it downtown. I could look for a place, a brownstone...and go for long walks by the lake. Maybe figure out a job for after my baby's born. I loved helping you raise Amy. Maybe I could take in kids or start a day care center."

"You'd be perfect at that." Molly beamed.

Bobbie's head spun with possibilities. "I could remodel your place, Mol. Then you'd be telling Danny the absolute truth."

Molly's blue eyes twinkled at the agreed plan. Dusk settled outside and shadows gathered in the kitchen they once shared.

Home is where the heart is and right then, Bobbie was home.

Molly pushed back from the table and took her purse off the kitchen counter. She zipped it open, dug inside and pulled out a key chain. In, out, no rummaging. She had always been able to do that and it never failed to impress Bobbie. Unlike Bobbie, Molly knew just what she needed and where to find it—directly, no detours. Bobbie would like to cultivate those qualities.

Molly sat down and handed Bobbie the keys. "I wish I could drive downtown with you, but Kay will bring the kids home in an hour and Danny should be home around then, too."

"I'd love to see them."

Molly frowned. "And they would love to see you, I'm sure. But I don't think that's such a hot idea."

Bobbie's disappointment gave way to logic. "You're right."

They stood, linked their arms around each other's waists and ambled to the front door.

"We could make up a story about you passing through and you could stay for dinner," Molly offered.

They reached the front door. Bobbie smiled. "And where would we tell them I'm going? It's better that Danny doesn't have a clue I'm in the vicinity."

"Yes. I'll talk to Amy. Figure out a suitable bribe."

Bobbie laughed. "If it involves money, let me know how much."

"You're covered." Molly opened the door and Bobbie stepped outside. "It was you, me and Amy against the world for a long time. I might tell her the truth. How do you feel about that?"

"I'm not sure. But you'll do what's best for her. You're the mom."

Molly smiled and touched Bobbie's middle gently. "So are you."

Chapter 18

Joe bounced the basketball with lazy pumps and eyed the competition. The Sullivans gathered at Kay and Mike's house for an end of the summer barbeque and the inevitable heated game was in progress in front of the house. He couldn't remember a family get together that didn't involve the lot of them trying to pound the crap out of each other with athletics as an excuse.

Meat roasted on the grill out back and flowers lofted fragrance on the warm breeze. The sun beat down on his bare chest and glinted off the sweat-streaked torsos of his brothers who squared off against him under the hoop in the driveway.

The ladies of the neighborhood did chores outside and watched the raucous game more than they paid attention to their work. He was aware of the audience and sensed that his brothers were, too, as he put the ball in play with a muscular pass and the men stepped up the action.

They loved to entertain the ladies.

Patrick intercepted Joe's pass and lined up a shot. Joe easily blocked it, but caught Pat's arm as he reached across to swat the ball away from the net.

"Damn it, Joe, that was a foul."

"Patrick! Language please," Jean Sullivan called out. His mother stood in the shade of the weeping willow that took up a large part of Kay and Mike's front yard. The wind ruffled her hair and she smiled at Joe, enjoying her family's antics.

"Sorry, Ma," Patrick said. Under his breath he cursed at Joe again, but watchdog Jean had excellent hearing.

"Patrick Sullivan do I need to go and get the soap?"

"No, Ma."

Mikey Jr. laughed at his uncle. "Nana caught you, Uncle Pat."

Patrick stood abashed at his mother's reprimand. Mikey seized the opportunity to dribble past his defenseless uncle and sink a lay up.

Kay came out the front door just as the ball swished through the net.

"Game over. Dinner is almost ready. Everyone in to wash up."

Joe picked up the ball and tucked it under his arm. He strolled up the driveway with his brothers, savoring their special time together. Family gatherings would never be the same without Jimmy, but his death had taught them not to take each other for granted.

They had seemed to seek each other out more often in the past few months—to touch base, draw tighter. It was hard to synchronize schedules so they could all be together like this, though.

"Great shot, squirt. We won." Joe high-fived Mikey and razzed Patrick, "Looks like we win for the third year in a row."

"No way. The game's not over. We'll pick it up after dinner," Patrick protested.

"No can do, sore loser. Brian and I have to get back to work after dinner. Guess you'll just have to wait until next year."

Joe grabbed his T-shirt off the lawn and mopped his sweaty face.

Dan pulled his shirt on and sidled over to Joe. "I haven't seen you in a while. How are things going? Are you happy to be back?"

"More than happy. I'm grateful every day. It's good to look forward to going to work."

"What are you working on?"

"We just nailed the Bike Path Rapist and I'm teaming up with Brian on that missing boy case. Maybe fresh eyes..." Joe huffed a laugh. "Make that a fresh eye, might pick up something missed."

"That case is cold."

"I know it. But the press won't let up and get off the department's case about the lack of leads. The brass are pissed."

The brothers ambled into the house and back to the kitchen where they tangled arms and bumped each other around over the sink.

"Mom, tell them to get out of my kitchen." Kay laughed as she shoved her brothers towards the door.

"Boys, listen to your sister. Go use the washroom. Kay is trying to get dinner ready in here."

"Where's Mike?" Joe asked as he wiped his hands on a paper towel.

"He called a little while ago. There was a pile up on the highway. Looks like he and Molly will be late if they manage to get home for dinner at all."

"I hoped I'd see Molly today," Joe said.

"Why?"

"I want to talk to her about something."

"Anything I can help you with?" Danny asked. He stood in front of the open refrigerator and gulped some orange juice straight from the container.

"No, thanks anyway," Joe said.

"Daniel, put that container back in the fridge or get a glass." Jean flashed a look of disgust at Danny, the offender.

"Yes, Mom." He grinned and took another swig before he complied.

She shook her head and lightly swatted the side of Dan's arm. "Go out and help your father with the grill before he burns everything.

"Kay, honey, I'm going upstairs to help Mary and Amy with the little ones."

"Thanks, Mom."

Kay and Joe were left alone in the kitchen. Joe took a closer look at his sister.

"You okay, sis? You look tired."

"I'm fine. Mike hasn't been feeling great lately so I am worried about him. I want him to get a check up but you know doctors never take care of themselves. How about you? You look good. How's it going being active on the force?"

"It's great."

"Really? You don't look that excited."

"I am. Just a few things going on."

"Is that why you wanted to talk to Molly?"

"Yep. I wanted to ask her about Bobbie. Have you heard from Bobbie?"

"No, I haven't talked to her since Jimmy's funeral." Tears gathered in Kay's eyes.

Joe put his arm around her. "You okay?"

"Yeah." She wiped each eye with the back of her index finger. "Can't help it."

"I know." Joe opened a cabinet door, took out a glass and filled it at the sink. He handed it to Kay.

"Bobbie hasn't taken any of my calls for months," he said.

"I thought you were working with her wrapping up the Sterling case."

"She delegated it to another agent. I've been working with him."

"Oh. Then why do you need to talk to her?"

"No reason." The scene out her kitchen window ended Joe's line of conversation. "We better get out there before Dan and Dad burn the hot dogs," he suggested.

She smiled and opened the sliding door that led to the back yard.

A pungent cloud of smoke wafted into the kitchen.

"Too late." She laughed.

****

Joe's eye blurred as he went painstakingly through every phone number on the suspect's last cell phone bill. The team had already checked the numbers but Joe wanted to go over it once more. He had a gut feeling that everybody had missed something.

They needed a break. No one held any hope of finding the missing boy alive. It had been too long and the odds against it were overwhelming, but the boy's family deserved to know what had happened to their son.

Joe rubbed his rough hands over his face and stared at the dingy phone on his desk. He picked the receiver up—then replaced it. How many times in the past few months had he called her? He had lost count of the rebuffs. She didn't want to talk to him—that much was obvious. But had he worked hard enough to find out why?

He was as restless and dissatisfied as he had been before he forced his partnership on Bobbie in the Sterling case. He had strived then to get back on the job, to fix everything and restore his old life.

Work was good, but when he went home at night, he was still alone and as unhappy as he had been when he pushed papers around for a living. Maybe, he was unhappier. Life was better with Bobbie.

He shouldn't bother her. He hadn't seen her since the day she had dragged her suitcase out the door behind her after she had proclaimed they were even. At the time it seemed right to let it go at that.

He saved her life; she saved his. She wanted to move on with David—he wanted his old job back. They had been straight with each other, no obligations.

He was proud of the work they did together and hadn't needed her to give him false credit for stopping Becky Adams. He couldn't prove it, but he might have been returned to active duty regardless.

He had hoped that tying up the case would have brought them together again. But she put John Donaldson in charge and had sent her statement to the arraignment with him. Joe had left messages for her at work and at home, but she had never called him back.

He missed her more than he could have ever imagined. A hole loomed large inside him that he couldn't begin to fill with work or anything else. Love? It had to be, although it had taken him a while to admit it and because he loved her, he wouldn't mess up what she had going with David.

Was he unselfish enough to let her marry David? What did she see in that jerk anyway? He had to prevent this. He needed to talk to her one more time, to convince her to choose him. He could make her happy. God knows she had made him happy, even if he hadn't shown her or told her. He'd figure out a way to let her know now.

If she told him to his face that she wanted David and not him, then he would wish her a happy life and try to move on.

He had made a good start toward the future he wanted with his job. Was it everything he hoped it would be? No. He needed love. He needed Bobbie.

He dialed the memorized number. A man answered.

"David?" He took a stab.

"Yes, this is David."

"It's Joe Sullivan."

"I'm sorry, I don't recognize the name."

"Well, hey Dave." Joe laid on the southern

drawl.

"Oh you. What do you want?"

"To talk to Bobbie. Can you please tell her I'm on the phone?"

"No, I will not tell Roberta anything for you."

"Don't be juvenile, Dave. Put her on the phone."

"She isn't here."

"It's Saturday. Is she at work?"

"No."

"Undercover again?"

"I have no idea. Maybe. She doesn't live here anymore."

"What?"

"She moved out months ago."

"Moved out? Why are you at her apartment then?"

"None of your business."

Joe's frustration mounted. "Where did she go?"

"She didn't say."

"I don't believe that." He pushed a pencil down hard on his blotter and the point broke off and flew somewhere on the floor.

"Too bad."

His patience strained to the limits. "Can you let me have her father's phone number then?"

"Father wouldn't talk to you. He doesn't know where she is either and let me tell you, he is furious."

Joe's gut twisted with worry. "Well if she calls you, can you please let her know that I am trying to reach her?"

"I doubt she'll call me, Joseph. Good bye."

He listened to the dial tone. Dave probably wouldn't tell him anything even if Bobbie had been standing in front of the prick the whole time they were on the phone. Still, he didn't get the feeling that Dave lied to him. The jerk didn't know where she was, either.

She had obviously dumped Dave. Given this new

chance, Joe laughed, elated, and dialed the New York Field Office.

"Hello. Special Agent John Donaldson, please."

"Speaking."

"Hey, John. I knew you'd be there on the weekend. It's Joe. Joe Sullivan."

"Sir, it's good to hear from you."

"Call me Joe."

"Thank you, Joe."

"How's the promotion going?"

"It's great, sir."

Joe smiled. John couldn't sustain treating him as an equal.

"Do you still work with Leighton?"

"No sir. Bobbie... uh, Special Agent Leighton resigned."

"Resigned? When?"

"It must be three months ago."

"Do you know why?"

"No. She told me goodbye and to be safe before she packed up her desk. But she didn't tell me or anyone her plans."

"That's strange."

"Tell me about it. I called her a couple of times and left messages. Finally there was a no-longer-in-service recording on her cell phone and I gave up."

"If you hear from her can you tell her I'm looking for her?"

"Yes, sir, I will. Is everything okay, sir?"

"Sure it is. Talk to you soon, okay? Be safe, John."

"You too, sir."

Joe stared at the wall across from his desk. Bobbie resigned? Disappeared? What was going on with her? She loved her job. Why would she quit? He hoped that her reputation hadn't suffered because of their conflicting reports of the Adams shooting. Nah. That would have come out months ago. *Where the hell is she?*

He skimmed the missing boy's file and dread shimmered through him. His new mission was to find both of them.

****

Molly peeked inside the bakery box and raised her eyes to meet Joe's.

"You brought me a chocolate Eli's cheesecake? Oh yum, screw the diet." She put the box down on her desk and squinted up at him. "You must want something. What is it?"

"You hurt me." He struck a melodramatic pose, his hand over his breastbone. "Can't a brother bring his favorite sister-in-law a treat without an ulterior motive?"

"Your only sister-in-law and no, I know you. You want something. Watch out or I'll get Danny over here to interrogate you." She laughed, her eyes filled with adoration.

"Whatever it is, yes. You know I'm a sucker for you boys. Spill it. As long as you don't want prescriptions for illegal substances, I'll give you whatever you want."

"I need to find Bobbie," he said, his gaze earnest and serious.

"Bobbie?" She paused and broke eye contact with him. "Why do you need to find her?"

"I need to talk to her. I've been trying to get in touch with her off and on and she's refused my calls. Now, none of her contacts in New York know where she is. She's resigned her job. I'm worried about her."

"Don't be." Regret flashed on her pretty face. "I'm sure she's fine."

"You know where she is. Tell me, Molly."

"Yes, I know where she is. And I know she's okay. That's all I'm going to tell you."

"Please tell me where she is."

"I can't, Joe. She needs time to herself. You hurt her."

"I hurt her? How?"

"That's between you and Bobbie."

"Then let me talk to her. How can I find out how I hurt her if I can't talk to her?" Joe stood and paced around Molly's cramped office.

"I can't betray a confidence. I promised I wouldn't tell anybody where she is," she asserted, her expression grave.

"I need to see her Mol. I have to let her know what an ass I have been. If it's not too late I want to make her love me. Please help me, Molly."

"How do you plan to make her love you?" Her gaze dropped to her hands then up to his face. "I'm sorry, Joe."

"I love her, Molly. Plain and simple, I am in love with Bobbie Leighton. That's the first time I said it out loud and it feels great. Maybe I should jump up and down on your couch." He beamed at her and then burst out laughing.

She registered surprise and when he didn't stop laughing, she joined him. Then her expression turned serious. "I wish she knew that."

"You have to tell her." The soft look on Molly's face convinced him that he'd made progress. "Better yet, just ask her to give me five minutes—better make it ten. I'm a slow talker."

"I don't know."

He clasped her hands. "I'm begging here." She wrestled with her conflicting loyalties.

"All right." She smiled. "I'll tell. But if you hurt her again, I'll kill you."

"I don't intend to." He held his breath.

"She's living downtown in our condo. In the Sterling Building on LaSalle and Kinsey."

"Sterling?" He blew air out of pursed lips. "Kind of figures."

He leaned over her desk and pecked Molly on the lips. "Thanks, sis. I owe you."

Chapter 19

Swollen feet, back aches, and utter exhaustion didn't alter Bobbie's newfound happiness. She left the paint, wallpaper and rug sample books on the glass dining table. Her arms twitched from the strain of carrying them from the car, through the lobby and during the elevator ride up.

She flexed her hands and rolled her shoulders. What a wonderful day with the real estate agent and then a stop at the Merchandise Mart showroom to gather some ideas for Molly's condo on the way back. With any luck she would be decorating her own home in a few weeks.

Foraging in the fridge, she selected a pitcher of iced herbal tea and gulped down two glasses, one after the other.

The phone rang and she answered, "Hi Mol. I think I found a house!"

"It's Annette, not Molly. That's so cool. Can I see it, too?"

"Sure you can. It's a brownstone within walking distance from Lincoln Park. It even has a little patch of yard in the back. I think it will be perfect for us. I didn't keep much of a poker face with the agent."

"Sounds amazing. I can't wait to see it."

"You'll be one of my first guests."

"The reason I called is I made a huge pot of turkey chili this morning. My family was supposed to come to dinner and I was just called into work, so I had to cancel with them. Want me to bring some over for you?"

"I would love it. I'm always famished. I'll come over and get it."

"Don't bother. I'll drop it off in a few minutes on my way to work."

"Okay, thanks. I'll leave the door unlocked."

Bobbie smiled as she unlocked the door. *How lucky I am.*

Molly and Annette took turns checking up on her. Cosseted by their affection, her strength grew and the pain of not having Joe in her life faded. She rolled out of bed each day happy with her plans for the future.

She couldn't wait to meet her baby, be a mother. As her due date neared, she missed her mom, would have liked to ask her so many questions. How had she reacted when she found out that she was pregnant? Had she been as excited as she was now? Had the rest of the world simply no longer mattered?

Bobbie carried her glass over to the table and sat heavily on the chair, delicious to be off her feet.

I should go through these samples before I see Molly tomorrow. If Molly had enough time, Bobbie planned to take her over to the brownstone for her opinion. Molly's agreement about how perfect it was would be all she needed to go ahead and make an offer.

Thank God for her mother's trust fund and the means to take this time to prepare a home for her child, her mom's grandchild, without worry. What a priceless gift.

Leaning over the table, her head on her arms, she debated heading into the bedroom, but didn't have the energy. Hunched over, she slipped into a light doze.

Bobbie had a recurrent fantasy about her baby, certain that despite Doctor Molly's opposite opinion, it would be a girl. A miniature Joe, dark curly hair, shimmering crystal blue eyes, a real daddy's girl that could twist him around her pudgy little finger. One look at his baby girl and he'd be mush.

Annette's light tap on the door brought her out of the pleasant daydream.

"Come on in. It's open."

"What the hell is the matter with you?" Her head snapped up at the angry male voice.

Joe stomped into the condo and slammed the door. "Didn't you learn anything on the streets? Are you crazy? You leave your door unlocked in the middle of the city?"

Her senses cleared and she knew she hadn't dreamed Joe into her living room.

"How did you find me?" she yelled.

****

Appalled that he could just waltz in while she slept, completely vulnerable to attack, he'd lecture some sense into her. She could be robbed, raped, even... He shuddered before going any further with that line of thinking. "I'm here to protect you since you obviously aren't doing it yourself."

"You're crazy. I don't need you to protect me, Sullivan. Get out of here." She spread her arms over the table, lowered her head.

"You ought to know better. Are you listening to me? Bobbie?" he demanded.

She raised her head. "Think back." Her tone dripped with disdain. "Who let trouble in? Not me. Who do you think you are, barging in here yelling at me? Get out."

He dodged just in time for the glass to miss the middle of his forehead. The woman had faultless aim.

Tense, he waited, certain she'd find something

else to launch his way. He smiled, detecting that devilish gleam in her eyes—the one that had preceded her jumping him and loving him senseless on the penthouse floor.

"Here we go again, Bobcat. Remember what happened the last time you used me for target practice?" He moved closer.

She gave no indication she remembered. A knot tightened in the pit of his stomach at the memory. He had been helpless under her spell, bewitched into wanting nothing but more of her. He hadn't forgotten. Had she?

He advanced toward her and then stopped short as she heaved up from the seat, "Wow, you got fat...uh, I mean, you gained a little weight and you look terrific."

The sarcastic look in her eye belied her laughter. "You're an idiot, Joe," she sneered.

"I'm sorry. You look great anyway. I better shut up before I put my other foot in my mouth."

"I'm not fat. I'm pregnant."

He slapped his hand down on the counter that separated the kitchen and the living room. "Pregnant! That son of a bitch! I'll kill him."

"What the hell are you talking about? Kill who?"

"David. That smug little shit. Did he break up with you, refuse to marry you?"

"Of course not."

"I could never understand what you saw in the guy, but I figured it was your choice."

"You're right, it was."

"He should be a man and take responsibility for his actions," Joe continued the rant. "He doesn't know how lucky he is. He doesn't deserve you or this baby."

His heart twisted. *As if I deserve you.*

"David is not my baby's father."

"What?"

"You heard me. David is not the father. I left

him, not the other way around."

Silence stretched between them.

Then the truth hit Joe like a canon blast. "Me?"

She nodded and sucked in a breath that hitched in her throat, her huge eyes pleading with him to do....what?

Elation soared. "Oh my God. I'm going to be a father? Why didn't you tell me?" As tears brimmed in his eye, he didn't care what her motives were.

Staggered with gratitude, Joe enfolded her shaking body in his arms. "Thank you." He kissed the crown of her head. "This is amazing."

Swamped with emotion, he vowed, "I'll take care of you. Marry me."

She shook her head, her eyes sad. Rosy hair fell over her shoulders. Her full breasts swelled over the shelf of her rounded stomach that sheltered his child. He seized her hands but couldn't find words.

Joe took off his eye patch and handed it to her.

Tears streaming, she covered her mouth with one hand.

"Here I am," he said. "This wasn't your fault but I blamed you...or maybe it was easier to blame you than risk being rejected by you. I'm sorry it took me so long to figure things out. Because I love you, Bobbie. Maybe I always have. I believed that finding Jimmy's killer would set things right. Returning to active duty would give me back my old life. Nothing changed. Jimmy's gone. Something was still missing. You, Bobbie. I don't want a life without you. Please, Bobbie. Marry me."

"Are you sure you're not just asking me because of the baby?"

"I'm sure. I love you, this baby and all the babies we'll make."

She covered her eyes, bent her head and sobbed.

It broke his heart. "Please don't cry." He hugged her close.

"I love you, too, Joe. I always have."

He sealed her lips with his, a kiss that spun on, tender as their unborn child, sensual as bobcat fire.

She guided his hand to her abdomen. A knobby bump poked it, rolled and shifted beneath his fingers and then fell away. *My child.*

"We say yes." She kissed his scar, the softest intimacy.

"Ah, Bobby."

Why didn't I plan this better? "I don't have a ring to make this official," Joe said. "We can go down to Jewelers' Row on Wabash and you can pick out anything you want."

"Anything?"

"You name it."

"I want a hot fudge sundae."

"You don't want a ring?"

"Eventually." She kissed him, hard, teasing. "We can come back here after we get ice cream and I'll throw plates at you until we wind up in bed."

"I'll tell the family to buy us plenty of dishes for our wedding."

She snorted indelicately.

Laughing, Joe swept her hand up, kissed the finger where his ring would go and wondered why he had ever wanted his old life back.

K.M. Daughters

Thank you for purchasing this Wild Rose Press publication. For other wonderful stories of romance, please visit our on-line bookstore at www.thewildrosepress.com.

For questions or more information contact us at info@thewildrosepress.com.

The Wild Rose Press
www.TheWildRosePress.com